Two Houses

by

Heidi Peaster

All Rights Reserved

This is a work of fiction. All characters, places, businesses, and incidents are from the author's imagination. Any resemblance to actual places, people or events is purely coincidental. Any trademarks mentioned herein are not authorized by the trademark owners and do not in any way mean the work is sponsored by or associated with the trademark owners. Andy trademarks used are specifically in descriptive capacity.

This is a work of fiction. Names characters, places and incidents are products of the author's imagination or are used factiously and are not to be construed as real. And resemblance to actual events, locations, organizations or person, living or dead, is entirely coincidental.

ISBN-9781-4751-89865

Copyright 2012
Second Edition 2014
By: Heidi Peaster
Photographs by: Cody Peaster

6

Two Houses

1903—Dooley, Georgia

Brynn decided, even as cold as it was that January day, she was going to go ahead up to Old House as she had planned.

She had been waked up early by her niece. She and two year old Amelia shared a room down at Sister Kate's, which was never a very comfortable reality, but today, although it was Saturday, she didn't mind being waked early. On school days, she was up before her niece, up and helping Katie with breakfast before meeting the twins and Sorrel to walk to school.

Usually on a Saturday, even if Amelia decided to get up early, Brynn was able to hunker down under the covers and pretend to be asleep until Katie came to get the little girl up, then drop back off. But today, it didn't matter. She had plans today.

She still helped her sister with breakfast this morning, although Kate told her she didn't have to. "For heaven's sake, Brynnie," she told her. "Go find something fun to do. It's Saturday, after all."

Brynn told her that she would. She told her that she was going to take Angelina out and ride awhile. "But I'll be back to help with the baking," she assured her.

Saturday was always baking day. It was also the day when all the food for Sunday would be cooked so that no one had to light the stove except for making coffee in the morning before church. Her Uncle Kevin said that it was a throwback tradition from the Quakers. No work done on Sunday. Aunt Janny said that whatever it was, she liked not having to cook one day a week, even if it meant doubling up on Saturday.

She knew if she left early enough, she could avoid everybody else. Buck was up and at the barn, of course.

Uncle Kevin, too. Aunt Janny had already cooked breakfast for him and sent him on his way. But Brynn didn't have to talk to them. Even if she saw them in passing, they would just say Good morning and let her go on her way. They knew she had things to do.

She made up her bed hurriedly after she helped get the biscuits in the oven. Going out through the kitchen, she dropped a kiss on Amelia's head as she sat in the high chair, and grabbed her coat and scarf off the rack, dashing out into the cold.

It had been four months since her mother and father had died and the whole world changed. Sometimes she still woke and, in that foggy, drowsy place before she opened her eyes, she thought that she had dreamed it all and her mother was downstairs cooking breakfast. She would be cooking and her daddy would be getting his coffee, standing near her mother to drink it before his first trip down to Long Barn to get the milk.

In that drowsy place, Brynn would smell bacon cooking and hear her parents talking quietly together the way they did so as not to wake the children. She could almost see them. She could almost see her mama look over at her daddy and he would smile at her in his teasing way.

Then, the next instant, she would remember where she was. She would remember that she was at her sister's house, that mama and daddy were dead and in the graveyard at church and that Old House was standing empty, waiting to be sold.

This morning, that was where she was going. She was going to Old House. She had stayed away long enough, she decided; long past when the doctor had told them. Now it was January and very cold and the house would be very cold, too, but she was going. And she was going to decide, once and for all.

Angelina was ready for a run. She managed to avoid Uncle Kevin and Buck, Taylor and Clay and saddle her quietly in her stall. Angelina was a beautiful horse; the most beautiful that Brynn had ever seen with her blue-gray Appaloosa markings and her tapered face. She was eager to get going, but she stayed quiet as Brynn led her carefully outside and mounted her.

She didn't know why she thought she had to be so secretive. Her uncle and aunt and cousins wouldn't care if they knew she was riding her, or even where she was going. But, somehow, knowing the plans that she had in her head, Brynn thought it was best to stay secret. Until they had to know, that is.

Old House was just the same. It was still not neat and tidy like New House or Buck's house from the outside. It was cranky. That was what Jordan always said and Brynn thought that he was right. It was dark with age, all odd angles and rough wood board and batten on the outside. The back steps were buckled in places as they led up to the back stoop near the elm with the coming home bell hanging from it. Brynn left Angelina at Long Barn and climbed the hill to the rise where the house stood.

There was the clothes line where her mother had hung line after line of clothes on a washday. Amy had always liked washday. Brynn had liked it too. She had loved the smell of sunshine on the clean clothes; she had loved how sheets sounded when they cracked in the wind. She went up the steps to the stoop and reached over the back door lentil for the key to let herself in. And, then in a moment, she was inside.

She stopped just inside the door. The feel of Old House closed all around her as she stood there, then, as she shut the door and walked further in, the sound of her shoes on the bare floor woke the echoes. There was still that smell of sulfur, but it wasn't strong. Sulfur and lye and stale air, she thought.

She looked at the table where they had all sat to eat, at one chair slightly askew, and at the window seat and at the

Lintel

stove with wood still in the box beside it. The door to her parents' room was closed. Through the doorway to the front room, she could see the beginning of the stair case and the mantle in the front room and a glimpse of her daddy's chair.

On an impulse, she went quickly to the window nearest her and opened the sash to the wintery air. It was no more frigid outside than in, and the biting air that blew in on the meager breeze was fresh and helped dispel the stuffiness. She thought about opening every one of the kitchen windows that bowed out toward the view over the grassland, then discarded that idea. She would just have to close them all back up again.

Instead, she went to the stove, opened the door and poked inside. It was cold ashes, of course. Looking about, she found an old newspaper, crumbled it up and stuffed it into the stove, then got the matches from the shelf where they always were and lit it. When it blazed, she got the kindling from the wood box and placed it carefully, tending it until there was a tidy fire. She sat down on the floor before it with the stove door open and watched it.

She had just about got it all straight in her head when there was a scrape of boot heels on the stoop and the door opened. Brynn didn't move except to turn her head and meet his eyes. She knew it was Boone, and so it was. He looked at her, then blew his breath out.

"So it's you," he said annoyed.

She didn't reply.

"Didn't know who it was up here building a fire and opening windows," he added, coming further into the room and closing the door.

Boone was tall and dark like their father and Brynn had thought him the very best brother there could ever be during most of her growing up. Now, she was seventeen, he was twenty-one and, although people said they looked too much like each other, they didn't think alike much of the time. But she loved him, anyway. He walked about the room, just as she had done, but he went further and walked to the doorway of the front room, then to the closed door of their parents' room. He even opened it and looked inside, then closed it and came back. She didn't watch him.

"So what are you doing up here?" he asked her. "It's cold as a witch's tit in here."

"I wanted to come," she replied, her eyes still on the fire.

"Why?"

"It's home."

"Not for long," he muttered, as if he didn't really want to say it.

"They're selling it," Brynn agreed. "Uncle's selling it."

Boone didn't say anything. He prowled the room again.

"Do you want them to sell it?" she asked him, still watching the fire.

"Nothing I can do about it," he said.

"Yes, there is."

"No, there ain't."

"Yes, there is," she said. She looked up at him. "If you want to."

There were some people who were afraid of Boone, she knew. People had been afraid of her Daddy, too, because he was dark and quiet and had eyes that no one could read. She had never been afraid of her Daddy, and she wasn't afraid of her brother, either as he stood there regarding her in silence. She knew she had puzzled him, so she just watched him until he asked:

"What are you talking about?"

Now was the time she had been dreading. She never knew how to really put things into words, at least not quickly. Not like Jerusha could with her rapid-fire retorts. Brynn had considered what she would say for a long time, and now everything she had decided seemed silly. But, she had to, so she said:

"They can't sell it if somebody lives in it." And looked at the little crackling blaze again.

"But nobody does," Boone replied.

"But somebody could."

"Who?"

"Us."

"Who us? Us who?"

"Us. Us children. You and me and Jordan and Jerusha and Sorrel. Us."

"Us live here? We live here?"

"Yes."

He came then and sat on the floor, too. He sat a little to the side and faced her, sitting Indian style. Brynn cut her eyes at him warily. He had a look about him.

"Brynnlin," he said. "What are you talking about?"

She took a deep breath and told herself that she would have to say it a lot more times than just this one, so she'd better get used to it.

"If you and me lived here," she said. "And I quit school and got a job and Jordan worked part-time at New House for Uncle Kevin and you help with what you make at Carson's…"

"Whoa, now wait a minute…"

"Just if," she went on doggedly. "Then we could all live here together and be a family. Here at Old House. Like it used to be."

"It won't be like it used to be," he told her. "And we ain't no family no more."

"Yes, we are," she said and this time, she looked right at him. Right at him. She didn't care. "We are a family. Just cause Mama and Daddy aren't here don't mean we aren't a family. We're Mama and Daddy's family. Morgan and Amy's. We're their children, not Uncle Kevin's and Aunt Janine's."

"I know that, but…"

"You know that and I know that, but if we don't do something, the children will forget," she said. "Jordan and Jerusha and Sorrel. They'll think they're Kevin and Janine's. So will everybody else. Everybody'll think that Clay and Adam are our brothers, not our cousins and that I'm just some poor relation living with Kate and Buck and I'm not even related to the children and neither are you because you don't even live on this side of the river. The children will forget that we're even brothers and sisters."

"Oh, come on, Brynn."

"It's true! You know it's true. We'll just be McKennas. Just a bunch of McKennas, lumped in with all the rest and nobody will remember that we're separate. We are separate, Boone. We're Morgan's. We're Amy's. We're not a bunch of New House McKennas; we're an Old House bunch."

There was a silence, then he said slowly: "You're saying you want to quit school and bring the children up here to live with you and me? And you think you and me can make enough money to support all of us up here? Live here and work and take care of the twins and Sorrel? Is that what you're saying?"

She nodded. She couldn't say it any more.

"That's insanity."

She said nothing.

"What kind of job could **you** get?"

"There's a job going in town," she told him. "Five days a week as a companion for old Miz Darcy…"

"That old hag? Good lord, girl…!"

"It pays pretty good and I figure I could get a raise soon if she likes me…"

"That old bat won't give you no raise, I'll bet my bottom dollar on that."

"And with what you make and if Kevin will pay Jordan part time," she dug in her pocket for the paper. "I figured it up. Groceries and such. See?" She pushed it at him. "That's how much we'd need."

Boone took it and smoothed it over his knee. The fire popped loudly, making her jump. After a minute, he said, still reading: "Kevin will never go for this."

"He might."

"He'll never let those children out of his house. Never. Especially for a hare-brained scheme like this," he looked at her again. "Brynn, this is crazy. You can't raise three children."

"You'll be here."

"I can't raise three children, either!"

"The twins are thirteen now. Sorrel's nearly twelve. They're not babies. They can go on to school, then come home and start supper and then we'll come home and finish and they can do their homework and go to bed. On the weekends, we can clean house and wash the clothes. I know we can." She could do nothing more than look at him. "I know we can, Boone. I know it." There was a soft sound outside the back door and Tommy, the maine coon cat, jumped through the open window. She came immediately to them and sat down, facing the fire. Curling her tail about her paws, she began to purr. "I just know this is right," Brynn said at last.

"You'll have to get past Kevin," he said.

"Well," Kevin said, beginning to light his pipe. "This looks like serious business."

Brynn glanced at her brother sitting next to her, but Boone didn't return it. Her Uncle Kevin pulled the flame from the match into the bowl of his pipe and flared it back up with its squeaky, puffy sound. Blue smoke billowed. She had always loved her uncle's study and had never felt intimidated sitting across the big desk from him. Until now.

"Uncle Kevin," she said at last. "We need to ask you something." Boone mumbled and she amended: "I need to ask you something."

"All right," he replied. "Go ahead."

The two of them were like peas in a pod, Kevin was thinking. Jordan and Jerusha didn't look more alike. Morgan through and through. Except that there was something very Amy about Brynn at times.

"Could we..? We want… Could we..? What I mean is," she said. "We really want to take the children and live in Old House now. And not sell it. Live in it. All of us. Me and Boone and the twins and Sorrel."

Kevin blew smoke in a rush, as if it had been pushed out of him. "Oh," he said.

"You won't have to pay for us to be there," she added hastily.

"Oh?"

"No. You won't. I—I've got a job," she said ignoring the sudden look Boone gave her. "I've got a job in town and with what Boone makes at Carson's and we were---I was thinking that you could maybe hire Jordan on part time down at New House…"

"Jordan?"

"Yessir. I know he's not very old, but you know he can do farm work and you wouldn't have to pay him much; just whatever you felt was fair."

She stopped and he was just sitting there, holding his pipe as if he had forgotten it. After a minute, he said: "Well." Then he said: "Well. Seems like you've been thinking about this for awhile."

She looked at her hands. "A little while."

"Brynnie," he said and when she switched her gaze up to his, he asked: "What's the reason behind all this, then?"

Again she glanced at Boone, then because she knew she had to, she replied: "It's just—I just---I don't want to have Old House sold, for one thing. And anyway, even if it wasn't going to be, I just want us to be a family there again. I know it won't be the same," she said quickly so he wouldn't. "But it's like---it's like we're all just scattered all over. All parceled out and lumped in with everybody else. It's not that I don't thank you for everything, Uncle, truly; because I do. For everything. But, well, we're Morgan and Amy's children. Old House children. I want to be a family in Old House. If we can." She was picking at her fingernails again, and she couldn't stop. They were ragged, but she couldn't stop. She watched herself do it so she wouldn't see the look on his face.

"We really feel," Boone said suddenly. "that this is what Mama and Daddy would want. They would want us to try for it. For awhile. Just to see if it's possible."

Kevin sat a minute, then remembered his pipe and sucked on it a bit. It was struggling to stay lit. "For awhile," he echoed. Both sitting across from him looked up at the words. "You said for awhile," he added. "How long are you thinking?"

Then, they looked at each other. "Maybe--," Brynn said slowly. "Six months?"

"Six months."

"Yessir. Or maybe through the summer. Till school next fall."

"You're talking about the rest of the winter, you know."

"Yessir. I know."

"We're coming up to the coldest part right now," he reminded her. "And March is worse than all the rest, sometimes."

"Yessir."

He pulled at his pipe, watching them in such a way that they knew he wasn't really watching them, but looking at nothing. His pipe had no smoke coming from it at all now, but he didn't notice.

"You talked to the children about all this?" he asked at length.

Again, they looked at each other. "Uh---no, sir," Brynn said.

"Why not?"

"Well, I guess because I---we wanted to hear what you said first. Not get them all up in the air about it."

"What if they don't want to?"

"Then we won't, I guess," she said. "Not without the children."

Again he was silent. He realized after a minute that his pipe was gone out and began patting his shirt pockets for a match. Brynn reached across the desk and pulled two from the little box and handed them to him.

"Thanks," he said absently, striking it on the side of his desk. "We used to call these Lucifer sticks in the old days, did you know that?"

The two shook their heads.

"Well," Kevin said around the pipe stem as he lit it again. "First off, I need to say one thing to you. To the two of you." He waved out the match and blew a stream of blue toward the ceiling. He fixed them with a direct gaze. "I want you to hear this, both of you." They both sat quite still. "I never want you---any of you children---to think for one minute that you have to be thanking me for anything I've done since your parents died. You hear? Nor your aunt, either. Anything that's been done has been done because we want to. Not because we have to or that we want any thanks for it. Is that understood?"

"Yessir," Brynn said.

"Boone?"

"Yes, sir," he said.

"All right," their uncle went on. "With that said; if you talk to the twins and Sorrel and they go for this scheme of yours, then I think you can give it a try. Till September. Then, we'll re-evaluate the situation. If at the end of that time, you want to change things, then we will. If any time before then any of you have a problem with it, then we'll try something else. And," he added. "I want you to know that if you have any problem up there, you can come to me. Or your Aunt Janny. If you want to just talk, then come to either of us. Is that understood, too?"

"Yes, sir," they both said. Brynn's eyes were alight, he saw. There was a curve to her mouth that he hadn't seen in quite awhile.

"So, you better go talk to the children," he told them.

They both stood, exactly at the same time, with the same movement to them. But Brynn was the one who came around the desk, bent and kissed his cheek. She was really smiling now.

"Thank you, Kev," she said.

"You're welcome," he told her.

"You mean, live up there all by ourselves?" Jerusha asked incredulously.

They were all in the girls' room. Clay and Jordan slept in Adam's old room at New House, which was the biggest, but the girls' room, which used to be Clay's room, was more private. Jerusha was sitting with Sorrel up on the pillows at the head of her bed, Jordan was on Sorrel's bed, stretched out on his belly, half dangling over the side. Brynn came over to him and made him move over so she could sit. Boone had the only chair, making cat's cradles with one of Sorrel's hair ribbons.

"It'll be all of us," Brynn pointed out. "It won't exactly be 'by ourselves'."

"No grown ups," Jerusha replied.

"What am I, a baby?" Boone asked.

"You're just a brother."

"I'm an adult brother."

"Who'll take care of everything?" Sorrel asked in her big-eyed way.

"We will."

"Who'll cook?"

"Well," Brynn said. "I will. I can cook."

"Not chicken and dumplings. Not like Aunt Janny."

"Nor apple pie," Jordan added. "Nor beef roast. Nor---."

"We'll learn," Brynn told them firmly.

"Who'll wash our clothes?" Jerusha asked. "Or clean? Or iron?"

"We will."

"Who we?" she asked just as Boone had.

"All of us."

"That's a lot of work," Sorrel remarked. "With school and homework and all."

"And---um---Jordan?" Brynn said hesitantly.

The boy looked up at her.

"You'll be working for Kevin part time."

"I will?"

"Part time. After school and weekends and such. For pay. We'll need you to. And I'll quit school and get a job. With Boone's pay, we should be able to make do like that."

Jordan regarded her a moment, then a smile spread across his face. "Good," he said simply. "Except for one thing."

Brynn looked at him warily. "What's that?"

"I quit school, too."

"Oh, no you don't, Jimbo."

"Oh yes I do."

"Oh, no you don't. You can't quit school."

"Why not if you're going to?"

"Because you're just thirteen, that's why. Mama would have a fit."

"If I do, I can work full time," he pointed out.

"No."

"Make more money."

"No."

"All right," he said coolly. "If you don't say I can quit school, then I won't go along with any of it. And I'll pitch a fit and beg Kevin and Janny to not let y'all do it either."

"Jordan!" Brynn said, shocked. "You wouldn't do that."

He moved from his half-off-the-bed position and sat up. His mouth was very set. He looked way too much like Jerusha, Brynn thought. "Yes, I would too," he told her. "And they'd go along with me and y'all won't be able to get them to budge. And you know it."

"Aw, let him," Boone said, beginning on another cradle. "I was out of school before him."

There was a universal silence. Brynn glared at Jordan, then didn't look at any of them. Every time she explained it, it sounded more and more crazy. After a bit, when Boone had gone through three more cat's cradles, he let the ribbon drop from his hands and said to them: "So? What do you think? You game?"

"I am," Jordan said. "I want to go back home to Old House. You let me quit school, and I'm all for it."

The two younger girls looked at each other. Brynn knew what they would say. If Jordan said all right, then Jerusha would and Sorrel wouldn't be left out.

"Well," Jerusha said at last. "I guess so."

"Just give it a try," Brynn said. "Uncle Kevin says try till the fall and then we'll see if we want to go on."

"It's what Ma and Daddy want," Boone said. The children looked at him in surprise, just as Brynn had done. "They'd want us to try."

New House and Buck and Kate's with the Old House children had almost become normal since Morgan and Amy had died. It had become normal for the twins and Sorrel to walk to New House after school and for Janine to hand out cookies and milk and for Brynn to walk on to Kate's alone. The path up across the pasture and through the big farm gate that led to Old House was not so evident now. By spring, it would have been overgrown and faded away as the path from Long Barn up the hill to Old House back door would be.

 The ground beneath the clothes line at Old House would grow grass and then the grass would grow high and eventually, the house would look even more old. Kevin was right in his assumption that the time to sell Old House would be before that happened, while the house still looked habitable.

 In reflecting on his conversation with Morgan's children, Kevin decided that in fact, he had gotten very comfortable in having them where they now were. They had been absorbed into the respective households very nicely. They had settled, at least the twins and Sorrel had.

 Their grief about their parents' deaths seemed to have abated. There were no nightmares, no dark moods. Despite the fact that they were the ages they were, they were still sensible children; they laughed and did the chores assigned to them and went to school and, sometimes, talked about Morgan and Amy. Not often, but sometimes.

 They had stopped hankering after seeing Brynn and Boone all the time. Maybe that was good, maybe, he was beginning to think, it wasn't so good. Maybe, he thought, they were beginning to get accustomed to being just in his family and forgetting that their brother and sister were part of it. Forgetting wasn't exactly what it was, of course. He didn't know what it was, exactly. It just wasn't the same, and of course, it wouldn't be.

 He thought about the conversation the rest of the day. He didn't like the thoughts that it put in his head; he somehow felt that maybe he hadn't done the best for his brother's children, although he knew he had done the best he knew how.

 He watched Jordan at supper that night, at how he was so much like Amy, and like Jim, and how he teased his sisters; he watched Jerusha who was so like Amy in her hair and face and yet so unlike anyone he recognized; he watched Sorrel who was like Morgan sometimes even more than Brynn was; and wondered what else he could have done. What else could he have done but what he did?

More than anything, having Brynn and Boone sitting in front of him made him miss his brother and sister too much. He was tired of missing them. He was tired of the grief. He had settled, too, into this new way of life, and Brynn was about to upset it again.

Janine was too quiet for Kevin's liking that evening. He realized, too late, that he really should have consulted with her before he gave his blessing to Brynn's plan. Janny liked to at least be consulted, even if Kevin's ultimate decision conflicted with what she thought best. So, he watched her a trifle warily as she did all the usual things tidying up the kitchen.

She didn't do them any differently than she usually did---filling the coffee pot for the morning, wiping over the table one more time, folding the dish towels and hanging them straight on their racks---but there was a little tightness to her lips that he recognized.

They didn't speak of it until he had at last locked the back door, blew out the lamp in the kitchen and gone upstairs to their room in the shadowy dark. It was very cold. Folks were talking about this January being as cold here in the North Georgia hills as the Big Cold of twenty years before. Kevin himself thought it was too cold to be in the south. The summer before had been as hot as a summer in Georgia could be, but in the hills at least every night cooled down and most every afternoon brought a rainstorm.

They said that in middle and south Georgia, it was so hot as to be unlivable. Few people actually lived there now that the big plantations were gone these forty years. Kevin counted himself blessed to live in the hills. Even at the coldest times, even when the rare blizzard came, the weather moderated quickly. He hoped it would moderate for the children moving back up to Old House.

They both paused in the hallway. One of the boys was coughing. They stopped and listened, then when he settled, they moved on down toward their bedroom door. It was Clay. He had the end of a bad cold. So far, no one else had caught it, and the bothersome cough was the end of it. When they went into the bedroom and Kevin closed the door, he saw that look that his wife had carried all evening was intensified.

"That house up the hill is drafty," she said without preliminaries. She went to her dressing table and began pulling out her hairpins, laying them one after the other on the tray with a sharp click. One after the other. Click. Click. "Sorrel catches cold every winter up there."

"And she always gets over it," he reminded her. He was unbuttoning his shirt, pulling the tail out from his trousers. "Listen, honey," he said, deciding to take the bull by the horns. "I'm sorry I told them to go ahead before I talked to you about it. I don't know what I was thinking."

Janny was still very pretty, he thought as she met his eyes in the looking glass. There were a few lines about her mouth and eyes, a few streaks of gray in the red hair, and a more matronly curve to her, but she still had those auburn eyes that had so arrested him at the very first and her smile with the chuckle behind it was that of a born flirt.

Fortunately, she only used it on her husband these days, and only her husband knew she had the best bottom in town. As far as he was concerned, at least. Now, she was neither using her chuckle or her way of walking that he always found so fascinating. She regarded him as she undressed and got into her nightgown, and he gave her an open look.

"They're that brother of yours' children," she replied. "You can tell them what you want."

"Still," he said. "I'm sorry."

"All right," she told him, a little reluctantly. "But, Kevin, really. They're just children."

"Boone's twenty-one. Brynn's seventeen…"

"I realize that. But Brynn quitting school? Working for that Darcy woman? Why just a year or two ago, they were scared to death of her. As a matter of fact, so am I still. And how are they going to expect to keep house and have the children in school and everything that goes with it? What time will Brynn get home in the evenings?"

Kevin sat down and pulled off his boots, first one then the other. "I don't know," he admitted.

"What if one of the children gets sick and has to stay home? Who'll stay with them?"

"I don't know."

"And Boone. He's been on his own for years now. How will he like suddenly having to be home every night, looking after three children, being responsible for them, giving all his pay over to running a house?"

"I don't know," Kevin told her, shedding the rest of his clothes and doing exactly what he knew she would dislike; dropping them where they landed. He hesitated, then stripped off his long johns, too, and got into bed. It wasn't that cold.

Janine turned and gave him a look. "That's what I mean. Nobody has thought this thing out. Did you point any of this out to them? Did they have any answer to any of this?"

"No."

"No, they didn't have an answer, or no you didn't point it out?"

"No I didn't point it out," he admitted. He ran both hands through his hair. It was beginning to be salt and pepper among the brown of it, but at least he wasn't losing any. Yet.

"Kevin," she said.

"And Brynn won't be the only one quitting school," he added, deciding to tell it all. "Jordan says he's done. He wants to work here at New House full time."

She had picked up the brush, but now she put it back down with a clatter. "What? Now, that's ridiculous. He's all of thirteen years old."

"I know it."

"And you're just going to let him?"

"What do you suggest I do? Hog-tie him and hoist him into school every day? He won't learn anything if I do that."

"Tell him he has to go. Tell him you'll---you'll do something bad to him if he doesn't."

He yawned. "Such as what? Morgan gave up whipping the boy about two years ago. He said it didn't make any impression on him. He don't have anything to take away from him that hasn't been taken away already. He wants to help pay for this Old House thing."

Janny took up the brush again and brushed her length of hair with a vengeance. "Then tell him you will give him a horse if he'll stick it out one more year. Two more years. You'll give him his own horse and if he doesn't stay in school and make an effort, you'll take it away again. You know he hates working the farm. He always talks about how he's going to leave and do anything else. And putting the responsibility on him is unfair at his age. Kevin," she said, setting the brush away and coming to climb into bed. "why didn't you say all that to him?"

"Can't say as I thought of all that, actually," he replied.

"Make him finish out the year," she told him. "You know Amy wouldn't stand for him quitting at his age."

He sighed. It made him uncomfortable, her saying that. "I know," he said. "You're right. All right, then, I'll tell him. I'll tell him I won't pay him more than part-time, and I won't allow him on the property till after school time. And, if he stays in school, I'll give him a horse."

"Good," she said.
"Can we go to sleep now?" he asked.

-2-

"This day, we moved back into Old House," Brynn wrote in her journal. She stopped and thought a minute, then added: "just like Mama and Daddy would have wanted us to, so Boone says. I think maybe so, too. I hadn't thought of that when I decided it, but I think maybe so."

She closed it and slid it into the cubby hole in Amy's desk. Going out into the kitchen, she looked at all of it again. There was a fire in the stove and the kitchen was warm. It would be the only room that would be warm most of the time, she knew, for coal was dear and wood was scarce; at least wood that was sawn and split.

The woodpile was low. Usually by Christmas, her Daddy would have made several trips to the forest and cut and split it all until it was banked high against the wall outside, but not this year. He had died in the early fall, before he could make his first trip with Kevin and Buck. Nobody had thought that Old House would need a woodpile this winter.

From upstairs she could hear the three younger ones bumping around, unpacking their things back into their old rooms. Sorrel laughed, a sound that was so familiar but had been so rare the past few months, that suddenly Brynn felt as if her mother should be coming in the door.

She should be coming in and then, hearing Sorrel, she would be saying: "Listen to that child, Morgan. She laughs so hearty, doesn't she?" It all felt that way. As if Mama and Daddy should be walking in right now, any minute. In a way, it made the missing of them worse, as if it had all happened just yesterday.

Resolutely, she went to the box of provisions that she had brought up from New House. She hadn't really wanted to take anything from her aunt and uncle, since the idea was that they would be doing all this themselves, but her Aunt Janny had insisted. Just to tide them over, she had said. Just till they could get a first paycheck under their belts and get to town for groceries. And of course Kate had pitched in and sent up milk and butter and cheese. And eggs. Brynn was grateful for the eggs. All three houses had always shared the cows, one of them was Old House's anyway and was already back in Long Barn; but she had forgotten about chickens. She wondered if she could get back some of her mama's layers. They would need chickens. Unless she could find that red hen, if she was still alive. Buck had said that she had raised a brood in the fall, but that they had all run off to the woods and probably the coyotes had got them. They needed chickens.

She was unpacking and thinking that they would have to go to town for sure for beans and flour and salt, when the back door banged and Boone came in. He was ladened down with a box under one arm and a tied sheet bundle in the other.

"Get the door," he said and she did.

"How much money you got?" she asked him as he set down the box on the table.

"Why?"

"We need beans and flour and stuff from town. What's this?"

"Cornmeal," he said, pulling it forth. "And sour dough starter. From Carson's. Their cook, Ginny, sent it."

Brynn looked pleased. Cornmeal she hadn't thought of. Taking it to the larder, she pulled out the big barrel that had held the cornmeal for Old House and took off the lid. A few drunken miller moths flew out. "We'll have to scrub these," she said. "I suppose the flour is no good, either." Sure enough, the remnant in the bottom of the flour barrel was mealy. "Can you go to town for beans and such?" she asked over her shoulder.

"No," he replied.

"Why not?"

"Payday's Friday," he replied. "We'll have to make do till then. You talk to Mr. Darcy about that job that you told Kevin you already had?"

She came back out and put the starter jar on the window sill over the stove. "I did," she told him. It was one of the more frightening things she had done in her life. "He was very pleased with me, he said. He said I could start next week."

"How much?"

She told him and he nodded. "Reasonable, I guess," he said. "Not enough for me to be around that old bat, but it's your funeral."

"I named my price," she said. "And he said all right."

"Probably couldn't get nobody else to do it," Boone said. "You could've asked for twice as much."

She didn't answer. She wasn't looking forward to starting work for old Mrs. Darcy, although she liked her son and her son's wife fine. Mr. Darcy had indeed seemed relieved that she had come applying for the job. Just run some errands, he had said, and fetch and carry. His mother was getting on up into her eighties, he said, and couldn't get around like she used to.

She had a full time housekeeper and cook, but she needed someone young to be at her beck and call. Rosemary would do her meals, but his mother liked her tea of an afternoon, and if she could do that, too, that would be helpful.

Oh, and she liked for someone to read to her—would she be able to do that? Brynn had told him she could. She didn't like any of the modern books, he had added. Bible was good, and the classics. Brynn had assured him that she would read whatever she needed her to read. Five days a week, he had said, and how early could she get there? She wasn't looking forward to it. Still---she looked around the kitchen, heard the children upstairs, felt the warmth of the fire at her back---she would do it, and it would be worth it.

"So what's for supper?" Boone was asking for the second time, she realized. "Don't tell me you haven't started any yet."

"What time is it?"

"Time to eat."

"It's always time to eat as far as you're concerned," she told him. "Well," she said, going to the box Janny had sent. "there's new bread and, oh yum! Butter. And salt pork. And some potatoes. All right, we'll have fried potatoes and fat back and bread and butter. How's that?"

Her brother shrugged. "Have to do, I guess."

As she cooked, tying one of Amy's aprons on over her clothes, she thought about using a few eggs scrambled in, but they needed to save the eggs. Maybe they could have oatmeal for breakfast. Tomorrow was Sunday, they would have to go to church. They all needed baths that night, since they had church in the morning. They had to show Janny and Kevin that they could show up at church all clean, just like they were supposed to be.

She parboiled the sliced, peeled potatoes to cut down the cooking time, then set them into the sizzling fat and sprinkled them with salt as they fried. The fat back cooked with them and the smell filled the kitchen. She set the bread loaf on the stove to warm, dug out Amy's red-checked cloth for the table and got out forks and knives. She was humming to herself, happy that the table was set again, turning the crusty-brown potatoes onto the serving plate when she noticed Boone standing in the center of the room, looking at the table in silence.

"What's the matter with you?" she asked, forking up the thick slices of fat back and laying them beside the potatoes.

He looked at her over his shoulder. She usually could catch what he was thinking, but this time, she couldn't. "You set too many places," he told her.

"What?"

He gestured toward the table. "You set too many places," he repeated.

She looked and took a quick breath in. It was true. She had laid the table the way she always did; the way she had done it the last time they had had supper in Old House. She had laid her mother and father's places at the head and end of the table with the girls on one side, boys on the other. The way she always laid it when Boone came over from Carson's to supper.

"Oh," she said and quickly, before the children came down and saw, she took the two place settings away. Then she paused and asked: "Do you think we ought to sit at the ends, you and me?"

Boone gave her a look. "We're not married, us two. We're not the parents."

"I know, but…"

"You want to sit at the head of the table, go ahead."

"You ought to," she told him.

"Why?"

"You're the man."

"Nice of you to notice. But I ain't the head of any house."

"Well," she said. "You are, really."

"No, I ain't. If anybody is, it's you. This was all your idea, you know."

Brynn stood a moment, then went to the cupboard, put the extra plates away, then went and moved her plate and cutlery to the end. "There," she said. She had her hands on her hips, and looked at her brother. "Somebody has to be," she added.

The little ones didn't see the point in having baths. They didn't see the point in going to church, either, but she put them in their place. They had to go, she told them. It would be just the excuse Janny needed to come tell them that the Plan wasn't working.

"What plan?" Sorrel asked.

"The Master Plan," Boone told her with a grin. "The Plan that Brynnie's got."

"It's the reason we're here to begin with," Brynn replied in some exasperation. "Eat, Rue."

"These potatoes ain't cooked," Jerusha informed her.

"Mine are," Jordan said. "They're burnt."

"The reason we're here," Brynn said, ignoring them. "is that we're supposed to be living the way Mama and Daddy would want us to. And that includes church. That's one of the most important things. Kevin and Janine will be watching to see that we go to school—at least you three---and eat right, stay clean, and go to church. So we have to go. And you have to have a bath. You have to have a bath, anyway. I'd think you'd want to have a bath. You got school on Monday. You don't want to go stinky, do you?"

Jordan said he didn't care particularly. He wanted to quit, but he wanted that horse Kevin promised, too.

"Speaking of school," Boone said. "Not to put a damper on anything, but what's going to happen about next fall and Jerusha?"

They all looked at him, sitting next to Jordan. "What about it?" Brynn said. The potatoes were undercooked. But the fat back was good.

"She's supposed to go away," he said. "Virginia, remember? The scholarship's gone through and everything. Mama and Daddy wanted her to go."

"That's all changed, now," Jerusha told him.

"No, it ain't," Boone replied.

"Yes, it is. I don't have to go now."

"I thought Daddy said that you'd decided you wanted to go."

"Well, maybe I un-decided," she said. "I don't want to go now."

"It was what Mama and Daddy wanted."

"I don't care!" she burst out, across the table from him. "You shut up!"

"You shut up," he replied, mildly. "Don't get your knickers all in a wad."

"You two both shut up," Brynn told them. "We'll talk about it later." She knew her mother would never stand for them all to be saying shut up to each other, or shouting at each other at the supper table, saying knickers and things.

Silence ensued. When they'd finished, most of the fat back was eaten, and the bread and butter, but the potatoes were left. Brynn looked at them sitting on the plates as she cleared, weighed up pros and cons, and then decided to use what they left in something tomorrow.

She scraped them off the plates secretly, when the others were out of the room and covering them up, put the plate in the pantry. She was congratulating herself when Boone said from the pantry doorway:

"You think that would go over with Mama? Using scraps at the next meal?"

Brynn jumped, composed herself and replied: "Mama would say 'any port in a storm'. That's what she would say."

"Sure she would," he told her, letting her pass back out to the kitchen. "You want the big washtub in here for the little ones' baths?"

"Yes, please," she replied primly. "Boone?"

"What?"

"What **are** we going to do about Jerusha's schooling?"

He went outside the back door to where the big washtub hung on its hook on the wall, then came back in and set it in its place back from the stove. He waited until she pumped the biggest water kettle full at the sink pump, then hefted it to the stove to heat the bath water.

"Well," he said at last. "The scholarship will pay for room and board and matriculation…."

"What's that?"

"Teaching," he told her. "But she'll need books and copy books and pen and ink and…"

"All right, what else?"

"Train fare," he said. "to get there. And back. Eventually."

"Eventually?"

"Well, we won't be able to have her traveling back and forth from Virginia all the time," he said. "Maybe not for Christmas. Maybe not for the first summer, if we can find somewhere up there for her to stay."

"She'll have to come home for summer," Brynn said, rather shocked.

"Maybe," he said and even Boone was looking a little grim. "But she sure couldn't come home for Christmas."

They were silent then. After a moment, Brynn went and got towels and the soap pot and set them out. Going to the sink, she began pumping water in for dishes.

"We got till end of school to figure it out, anyway," Boone added. "Her teachers say that we need to let them know by then if she'll be going or not so they can let the school know."

Brynn nodded. Right now, she decided, she had enough to think about getting those three in the tub. She couldn't think past that.

They made it to church, although they were a little late because Brynn overslept. But, at least they made it, she told herself. Nobody had much to eat because the oatmeal had to be rushed and didn't cook well, and Jordan's stomach growled incessantly during the service.

Sorrel's eyes were red because she couldn't find her other stocking and had to wear the one with the holes in, but Brynn hardened her heart to her tears and told her that she was going to church if she didn't have any stockings at all.

They were just going to have to keep up with their own things, she told them as they rode in the wagon through the shivery January cold. Mama always kept up with everything, but Brynn wasn't Mama and she would be working and the younger ones would have to pitch in and be responsible for their own things.

The three in the back of the wagon were morose and quiet the rest of the way to the little Episcopal church. They presented themselves in the pew beside their Aunt Janny with a martyr-like attitude. Janny obviously thought that Sorrel had been crying about her mother, for she gave her a comforting hug and held her hand for the remainder of the service.

Brynn herself was more than a little thoughtful at the reminder that she would be starting work the next morning. She had never held a job in her life and the sight of old Mrs. Darcy's head in its black chapel cap up in her reserved pew made her insides curl. The straight back never bent or turned, even when the processional went by and everybody else bowed their head at the acolyte carrying the cross. Brynn tried not to look at her.

Instead, she knelt during the prayers and asked God to please, please let her be strong enough to do this, and to keep doing it. Lord, if this is what Mama and Daddy want, and what You want, please, please make old Miz Darcy be nicer than I always thought she was and make the children behave themselves and make Boone be a help. And if it isn't what You want.... She stopped then and couldn't think of what to pray for next. So she finished with; please let this be what You want cause we're in it now. Amen.

She still kept her head on her hands on the back of the pew before her, her eyes closed after she finished, until Boone punched her and she realized that they were singing the last hymn. Fr. Tim smiled at her as he passed during the recessional.

The next morning was worse than Sunday morning had been.

It was worse for a number for reasons. Supper the night before had been scantier than Saturday's supper had been, Brynn had slept very badly for most of the night and then had dropped off and slept too heavily and had only wakened when Boone yelled at her for the third time that they were going to be late.

The children's clothes were still topsy-turvy since they had done their own unpacking, and Sorrel was in tears again because this time she couldn't find the mate to her school shoes and had to wear her old ones. Boone told Brynn unequivocally that he was going to work and that she had to sort out all the problems of the morning because he, for one, was not going to be late. So, he left with the kitchen in a turmoil, catching Tommy Cat's tail in the door on the way out.

"I'm going to work, too," Jordan reported importantly, heading for the door.

"No, you're not!"

"Yes, I am. I don't care about the damn horse. I'm quitting."

"No, you're not," Brynn told him, whirling around from table to sink to laundry basket, trying to find all her own things. She hadn't had a chance to unpack, yet. "You're going to school like the others and going down to New House after. You know what Uncle said. He won't pay you but half a day, anyway, till school's out for the summer. And he won't pay you that unless you show him decent grades, so go."

"Sister, do I have to go off to school next year?" Jerusha asked her, brushing her hair in maddening slowness.

"Oh, Rue, for heaven's sake don't worry me about that now!" Brynn replied. "Go to school. The three of you are going to be late."

"Who's going to milk the cow?" Sorrel asked, sniffling.

Brynn stopped and looked dismayed. "Oh, my lord, I forgot," she said. "And look at the time."

"Leave her till we get home," Jordan suggested.

"You can't leave her," Brynn said. "She'll be miserable and go dry. All right. Rue, go milk the cow. The other two of you go to school. Rue, put the milk in the pantry and put the cat out and Jordan, you pour it in the separator when you get home from school."

"I'm going down to New House," he reminded her. "How'll I do that?"

"Well, you're not going to New House in your school clothes. When you come home to change, separate the milk."

"Why does Rue get to milk the cow and be late?" Sorrel said. "Why can't I?"

"Go to school!" Brynn howled at them. "Go—go! Where's my apron? And Jerusha, you better catch up to the others as soon as you can or I'll know the reason why."

She rode Angelina to Mrs. Darcy's house. She rode her harder than she would have liked to do, knowing that her hair was being blown about and wouldn't be as tidy as Mrs. Darcy probably would want, but she was not going to be late on her first day. Mrs. Darcy's house was on the other side of town, not too far from St. Jude's church, but quite a piece from Old House. Brynn would have enjoyed the ride, actually, because she took the short cut up over the back of town, a road that led uphill and had an overlook of Dooley's business district.

At the top of the hill, she pulled up and let Angy blow. She would have to walk her cool the rest of the way, late or not. Sitting quiet in her saddle, her own breath frothy and hurried, she rubbed her gloved hand on Angelina's gray neck.

"Good girl, Angy," she told her. "It'll be all right. Good girl."

She wished someone would say that to her, she realized a little ruefully.

Below them she could see much of the town. The closest was the Episcopal church, St. Jude's, and the churchyard where her mother and father were buried. It huddled under its stand of trees, the branches of the oaks twisting up and over. In summer, you couldn't see the gravestones, the canopy would be so thick.

To the west of the church began the business district of Dooley; the wooden sidewalks, the stores with their second story facades, the wagons beginning to rattle downtown. Further west, the courthouse could just be seen slightly around the corner, and the town square oaks reared up over the green where the bandstand stood. There were very few bands that played there, even on the Fourth of July, but the town declared that it was good to have a bandstand, anyway.

To the east of St. Jude's the east bridge rose on its unusual stone pillars. There were five bridges around Dooley and three of them were fashioned after the European hump-backed design. No one seemed to know who had decided that, but they were part of the landscape and were built in the same stacked stone as the old watch tower on the outskirts of town that was now part of the mill. The dam that made the mill pond with its picturesque waterfall through the sluice gate was stacked stone, too.

No one knew who had decided on the watch tower. It was on Carson land, beside the mill pond and was forbidden territory as far as the children of the town were concerned. It was unsafe, Carson said, and he had boarded it up. But, sometimes on Halloween, a brave or foolhardy boy would take it upon himself to do some "hain't-ing" of the old tower, climbing up the winding, rickety steps to swing a lantern from the slit windows.

Brynn couldn't see the tower from her vantage point, of course. It was far out of town, beyond the ford. But, as she urged Angelina down the hill, she had to cross the stacked-stone, humpbacked east bridge. She pulled her muffler up over her nose and mouth as rode up and over the bridge with its girth-high stone walls on either side. She suddenly felt a chill that was more than the January weather.

She knew exactly where the Darcy house was. Everybody knew where it was, because, since they were children, they had been told that the old witch lived there. The old witch was Mrs. Darcy herself and everybody knew that it was from her house that the thunder came. No one had dared, of course, to approach the house itself, but it could be glimpsed through its cloister of trees behind the graying, picket fence.

Brynn pulled up at the fence and made herself dismount before she could recall every odd detail that her brother had told them about Mrs. Darcy's weather-making revelries. She didn't believe any of it now, of course. But she still got down off Angelina, tied her to the fence, and took herself in through the gate quickly enough that she wouldn't remember them all.

The house wasn't big or imposing, nor tumbled and dark as any haunted house should be. It was just a smallish house, with trees pushing close about it, a wide porch and curtains at the windows. There was a curious knocker on the door and Brynn used this, hearing it sound inside the house itself. She took a quick peek at her watch and breathed a sigh of relief. She had three minutes to spare.

There was a step from inside and the door was opened by a tall, black woman in a white apron and turban. She looked at Brynn without speaking.

"Good-morning," Brynn said. "I'm Brynn. Mrs. Darcy---the young one---I mean, Mrs. Darcy's daughter-in-law---she said I was to come this morning to start work as Mrs. Darcy's companion."

The quiet, dark face didn't change expression. After a moment, she stepped back, opening the door wider and ushered her in. As Brynn came into the dog-trot hallway, a high-pitched, quavery voice called out:

"Rosemary, is it that girl here? Send her in, send her in to me."

Brynn looked over her shoulder at the black woman, but seeing no answer forthcoming, she walked toward the sound, unwinding her muffler. "Yes, ma'am, your son hired me and told me to come this morning." She walked across the short hall from the front door to the first room on the left that appeared to be the formal parlor and paused on the large hook rug in the center of the floor.

The room was lined completely with books.

At New House, in her Uncle Kevin's study, there were bookshelves from floor to ceiling filled with books and odds and ends, but nothing like she saw before her now. For a moment, it took all her attention. Every wall was lined with bookcases that reached nearly to the ceiling, and every bookcase was filled with books. The windows peered forlornly from the midst of the shelves; below each window was a seat padded and cushioned with pillows. Beside each window seat was a table on which stood a lamp and more books. Brynn stood still and gaped at it.

"Well, come in, then," said the voice and Brynn looked about for the speaker.

She located her with difficulty. There was a fireplace in the center of the far wall, a fire burning brightly, and beside the hearth, two chairs. In one, the far one, was Mrs. Darcy herself. Brynn took a deep breath and approached her.

"Good-morning," she said.

She was a little, birdy lady. She was dressed in what looked to be the same black dress that Brynn had always associated with her, one that fell to obscure her shoes, with long sleeves and a flounce of cuff to obscure most of the hands. One hand was in her lap, clutching a scrap of handkerchief in knotted fingers, the other gripped the head of a thin walking stick standing braced beside the wing-backed chair.

The white hair was pulled severely back into its bun and half-hidden under a black widow's cap. But it was the small, pale face with the arresting black eyes caught and held Brynn's gaze.

"You're McKenna's girl, are you?" the cracked voice asked.

"Yessum. I'm Morgan McKenna's girl. I'm Brynn."

"You're Brynnlin," she corrected. "And don't say yessum. It's yes, ma'am, if you please."

"Ye—yes, ma'am," she replied. Then, because she couldn't help it, she added: "But Brynn is my real name, not Brynnlin. Only my uncle calls me Brynnlin."

"Nevertheless," Mrs. Darcy said. "Brynnlin is the correct name. Brynn is a nickname for Brynnlin. And I don't approve of nicknames. How did you come?"

"Ma'am?"

"How did you come? What did you come on? Did someone drive you or did you walk or did you ride?"

"Oh," she said. "I rode. My horse is outside. Tied to the fence."

"Then go stable it," she told her. "A horse can't stand all day tied to a fence. There is a stable out back with two stalls. One is for my driving gelding. There is one free. Stable your horse, Miss Brynnlin. And don't put it away hot. And don't give it any oats, remember that."

"Yes, ma'am. No, ma'am," Brynn replied and stumbled over the edge of the rug as she went out.

She found the stable with no trouble. As she went around the side of the house toward it, she took a look at the outside, seeing what was commonly called an oriole window with carving above it, a back door out onto a tiny stoop, and two tall chimneys. The paint was peeling, but the eaves seemed in good repair, as was the stable itself, she saw as she got inside.

She paused a moment to take a breath or two. Somehow the little barn seemed homey and familiar after the house. A bay horse turned in his stall and put his head over the door in a friendly way. Brynn smoothed his face in passing.

The stall was a big, airy box with fresh hay on the floor and in the rick, and fresh water in the bucket. She unsaddled Angelina, took off the bridle and took the time to feel under her belly for sweat before she patted her and swung the door closed.

"Looks like they were expecting you, doesn't it?" she said in whisper. It was too quiet to speak aloud.

She hated to leave the stable, but she tramped resolutely back to the front door and this time, didn't knock, but walked right in.

"Scrape your feet!" the voice called out before she could close the door.

She complied and presented herself back in the front room, pulling off her gloves and stuffing them in her pocket. Mrs. Darcy was in exactly the same position as she had been and fixed her with a stern gaze.

"From now on," she said. "You will stable you horse and come in the back door at the kitchen. Then, hang your things where Rosemary shows you and report to me. Then, and only then will you be officially here. Make your arrangements so that you arrive here in front of me at eight-thirty each morning. Is that understood?"

"Yessum---yes, ma'am," she replied.

"Good. Go back to the kitchen, hang your things and come back. Are your shoes muddy?"

She looked down at them. "Uh, no ma'am, I don't think so."

"Make sure that they are not. Go on, now."

The kitchen was just as tidy and unremarkable as the front room was cluttered and surprising. Rosemary turned immediately from the large stove and led the way to the little cloak closet near the back door, opened the door and went back to the stove.

Brynn thanked her, hung her coat and muffler and, as an afterthought, took the gold locket that had been her mother's and dropped it inside the collar of her dress. Taking a deep breath, she went back.

The rest of the day would have been uncomfortable if it hadn't been so unusual to her. Mrs. Darcy liked to talk, which was convenient for Brynn was never much for talking to strangers. It didn't matter if she said anything or not, for Mrs. Darcy filled in all gaps. She needed things done for her constantly, from adjusting the cushions at her back to stoking up the fire. The fire was stoked often and Brynn learned that the little front room was to have the door shut to keep the heat in. Apparently, Mrs. Darcy felt the cold but Brynn was smothering hot by mid-morning.

"There's a draft somewhere in this room," Mrs. Darcy said. "No one seems to be able to find it, but it blows on my face. Let up the shade on that window and let the warm sun come in."

While it seemed that Rosemary was the primary housekeeper, Mrs. Darcy wanted Brynn to dust the front room and all the knick-knacks and oddities it held while she supervised. Brynn began to perspire under the big apron as she stood on the little step to reach the mantle.

"Now, be especially careful with that piece," she would say. "That was one my father brought from the far east. He was a sea captain and was as sea forty years. His father before him was a sea captain, too. Most of those ivory pieces are what he brought back."

At noon precisely, the door opened and Rosemary brought in Mrs. Darcy's luncheon. Instantly, Brynn realized that she was famished and hard on the heels of that revelation, she remembered that she had forgotten to pack herself any lunch.

Worse than that, she suddenly realized that she hadn't packed lunch for anyone. None of the younger children would have anything to eat. Well, she thought with a sigh, if they have to go hungry, then I will too.

"Brynnlin," Mrs. Darcy said. "You may have a half an hour for your dinner."

"Yes, ma'am," she replied.

She had nowhere to go, of course, and nothing to eat. Instead, she went out to Angelina and in the quiet of the little barn, she laid her face against the mare's warm neck, closed her eyes and was comforted.

It was dark by the time she got home.

As she rode the curve that led to Long Barn, she could see the yellow windows of Old House and something in her began to relax. By the time she had bedded Angelina, her legs were so wobbly, the long pull up the hill to the back door nearly did her in. If I can just get in the house, she thought wearily. If I can just get inside.

Inside the door, at first it was relief. It was warm. The warmth from the wood stove enveloped her. She took one deep breath. And then came the rest of it....

Jerusha was the first, of course. "Brynnie, what's for supper? I didn't get nothing for dinner and now there's nothing for supper."

Jordan added: "I didn't get nothing, either. And I had to work down at Kevin's after school and it was colder'n hell down there."

Sorrel came to her and said, with her eyes big in her thin face: "I tried to see what there was to fix for supper, but there just ain't nothing, Sister. No flour or nothing."

Brynn waded through them, stepped on something soft that squalled loudly and was the cat, and wrestled herself out of her coat. "Where's Boone?" she asked when she could get a word in.

Nobody knew. "Probably out having a high old time somewhere," she muttered to herself, going to the pantry door. "Well," she said aloud and looked at the empty shelves. "All right," she added and stopped again. She could feel the others behind her, watching her. "Where's the eggs?" she asked, at length.

"There," Sorrel pointed.

"All right. Scrambled eggs and cornbread."

They all groaned.

"That's all there is," she told them, gathering up the cornmeal and eggs and bringing them to the kitchen. "Take it or leave it."

"I want fried chicken," Jordan proclaimed.

"Want away, you won't get it," she told him, rolling up her sleeves.

By the time the cornbread was in the oven and she was beating the eggs in her mother's big blue mixing bowl, she had made a few plans. As she put in salt and pepper and a little milk which, mercifully, they had managed to remember to put into the separator, she outlined what she would be requiring of them.

"Rue," she said at the trio of faces. "Tomorrow, you are going to have to go to the Mercantile and buy some groceries. We'll make a list tonight."

"Good," Jordan said with conviction, getting out paper and a stub of a pencil. "I'll start. Sugar."

"Wait a minute…"

"And apples," Sorrel put in. "and if we get flour, we can make a pie."

"No, you don't," Brynn said. "Don't put that down…"

"How am I supposed to do all that shopping?" Jerusha demanded. "I can't tote all that home by myself. And where's the money to pay for it?"

"We have to have brown sugar," Jordan was saying to Sorrel. "And cinnamon."

"I'll be with you, Rue," Sorrel said. "I'll help you carry."

"I'm tearing up that list," Brynn told them. "So you may as well not make it."

"And we got to have more butter," Jordan went on. "and bacon for breakfast. And if we get raisins, we can have a whale of a pie!"

"Stop that!" Brynn said loudly. "Gimme that paper…"

She made a move to get to them and grab it, the bowl tipped dangerously, and most of the supper eggs went in a wash onto the floor.

Boone came in to a less than peaceful scene. Sorrel was crying, Jordan was using rather colorful language to describe his feelings, Brynn was matching it as she mopped up the mess with towels, and Jerusha was still protesting. The only one that seemed content was Tommy, who was lapping the milky concoction from the floor as fast as she could. Boone put the box he held onto the table and looked at them until they noticed him.

"Brother," Jerusha said to him. "Tell Brynn to stop."

"Good evening, family," he replied.

Brynn looked up at him from the floor, pushed a straggle of hair back, and looked again. "What's that?"

"Groceries," he told her. "You told me to get some, didn't you?"

"Groceries?" Brynn said.

"Groceries!" Jordan and Jerusha echoed, making a dive for them.

"Oh, look, Sister!" Sorrel exclaimed, pulling first one thing, then the next from the box. "Flour and sugar and beans and, and---."

"How the sam-hill did you get groceries?" Brynn demanded.

Boone took off his coat and replied: "Took the money and got it. Told Casey that I had to get off some early, went to town and got them. Got paid Friday."

Brynn sat down on the floor and looked at the cat. The others went on pulling out the dried beans and sorghum, salt and canned goods, even kerosene for the lamps. She watched them unearth each like it was Christmas. Boone stepped over her as she sat there, and peeping into the oven, asked:

"You want this cornbread out? It's bout burnt."

"Yes," she replied.

"What else is for supper?"

"This," she said, indicating the yellow pool on the floor.

Boone took the potholder, pulled forth the pan of cornbread and set it aside, before he looked at her. "That all?"

"Well, what the hell else do you think we have!" she shouted at him.

"We do now," he said mildly.

"You want to cook?"

"**I've** been working all day," he said. "**I** went and bought the groceries. Plus, **I'm** the man of this so-called house. That's not my job."

"Then the whole bunch of you can figure it out!" Brynn bounced up off the floor and slapped the towel back down into the eggy mass with a splat. "I bet nobody milked the cow this evening, did they? Didn't think so. And I suppose I'm supposed to do that, too. That's what I figured. So all the rest of you can have whatever the hell you want to! You decide!"

She snatched the milk pail from its hook and slammed out the door. Banging the door so that the glass rattled didn't quite help, so she paused on the step and slammed the milk pail at the coming home bell, hitting it with a clang. The pail bounded away down the hill. There was a momentary silence from the kitchen behind her, then the voices picked back up again.

It was good and dark by this time. The cold was worse than it had been the night before. Brynn stood a moment, then, with a sigh, she went down the steps and fumbled around until she found the pail.

She was examining the massive dent in the side when the door opened and closed again and Boone came down to meet her. He had his coat back on and when he got to where she stood, he took hold of the pail to take it from her.

"Let go," he told her, then, when she resisted giving it over, he yanked it free. "Gimme," he added. "Don't be an ass."

"What? You going to put yourself out and do the milking?" she said.

Boone looked at her. She looked tired, but he couldn't help that. He was tired, too. "Just go in and figure out about supper," he told her. "There's more eggs in there. I stopped by Kate's on the way home. I know, I know," he said. "But she had some to spare. And there's two laying hens in the barn. They used to be Mama's anyway; Katie gave them back for us to use. So go on." Then, when she still stood, he added: "I bought some canned peaches. We can have them for dessert, if you want to."

She was looking at him sideways and Boone wasn't totally sure but that she was going to take a swing at him. "Thanks," she said at length. "I'll make a cobbler. That won't take long."

"Good," he said and headed for the barn.

"Thanks, Boone," she added again. "And so when are you man of the house?"

Even in the meager illumination from the lamp-lit windows, she could see his grin. "When it suits me," he replied.

-3-

The pattern for the days that followed was not a totally comfortable one. But, Brynn decided, at least it was a pattern. She found that the easiest breakfast was cornmeal mush and she cooked it six days a week, even when Jordan insisted he was sick of it and then, one morning went and threw it up to prove the point. She told them all, right then and there, that if they didn't like what was for breakfast, then they could go without.

The children took cornbread for lunch, sometimes with a drizzle of sorghum in the middle, sometimes with smoked ham if they had it. Brynn took, for her own dinner, what was left over after she parceled out the children's. If they had apples, they divided them up. At least Boone got dinner over at Carson's as part of his pay. If there was anything he could squirrel away in his pockets and bring home, he did.

Once, he brought cookies for them, five of them. Brynn slid hers out of sight and then the next morning, Boone caught her tucking it, divided neatly into thirds, into the children's lunch pails. He handed her the cookie he had saved instead of eating it, and she divided that, too. They smiled at each other over the little deception, knowing how the children's faces would look when at noon they would find them.

Supper was not much more inventive, for it had to be something that Jerusha and Sorrel could put together themselves. Brynn couldn't bear to have to come home and start cooking, so she left them pretty much to their own devices.

Their mother had put up a lot of the vegetable garden's produce the summer before she took sick and the root cellar still had beans and tomatoes, okra and pickles on the shelves. It made for some interesting concoctions, but usually Brynn was so tired, she didn't care if she had eaten firewood, as long as it was hot. Then, there were dishes to do and homework to get started.

She deemed that it was fair for her to clean up the kitchen since the children did the cooking and so, while she scraped pots and presided behind a steamy curtain at the dishpan, they spread out papers and books on the kitchen table.

Boone usually did most of the helping with homework, thank goodness, for she felt as if her brain was freezing over by that time. At least he's good for something, she thought more than once, and then would realize that she was being a bit unfair. She knew, down in her soul, that if she didn't have Boone to take her side against the others, she never could do any of it.

"If the two of you don't stop fighting, I'm going to beat both of your butts for you," he would tell the twins, usually with a thump to the back of the head for each. Or: "Sorrel, quit your whining and get on with what Brynn told you to do or you'll be doing it and eating off the mantle afterwards." Somehow, Boone could say something like that and get more cooperation out of them than if Brynn shrieked like a fish-wife.

"It's all in the delivery," he told her with a grin when she complained that they never listened to her. "They know exactly what you will and won't do. They still don't really know with me, and I let them know that they don't know." To which Brynn declared that that didn't make any sense at all.

But even home with all the chaos was preferable to Mrs. Darcy's house.

She had settled into a bit of a pattern at Mrs. Darcy's, too, but the problem was that Mrs. Darcy kept changing it. The old lady was always up and dressed in her same black widow's dress and cap, her breakfast already cleared away by Rosemary, sitting by a fire that had obviously been lit hours before Brynn arrived, for the room was always smothery warm. Despite it being the coldest part of January, Brynn learned after the first week to dress as if for the mildest spring, for Mrs. Darcy's parlor was breathless.

Mornings were spent in cleaning, about which Mrs. Darcy was very particular, both in how it was to be done and also who was to do it. Rosemary was official housekeeper and therefore did the regular sweeping and dusting and mopping, as well as all of the cooking, except for Mrs. Darcy's tea at the end of the afternoon.

Brynn apparently was to do any extra cleaning that Mrs. Darcy took into her head had to be done that day---from taking down a bookcase full of odds and ends to be dusted, to polishing up the old-fashioned silver service on the sideboard in the dining room. Brynn wasn't sure which she liked least; fighting spiderwebs drifting their way about the knick-knacks on the shelves, or rubbing endlessly at the carved silver.

"Be careful of that, for mercy's sake!" Mrs. Darcy would tell her. "That piece of glass is older than both of us. Don't go tossing it down like that! My grandfather brought that from Asia ninety years ago, all the way around the Cape of Good Hope. You break that and you'll be working for me the rest of your life for no pay whatsoever."

It was also Brynn's job to keep the fire burning at maximum output, but this she liked much better for it entailed her going downstairs into the big cellar and bringing up the coal scuttle full at least three times a day. The cellar was a massive, dark labyrinth of stone pillars and shadowy corners with a sweet, chilly scent that, rather than being a frightening place, was mysterious and refreshing.

It also brought Brynn into Rosemary's realm, for the cellar steps led down from the kitchen and Rosemary, though she never spoke, always would turn from whatever she was doing to give her a nod. Brynn decided that she liked Rosemary, even if she never responded to her Good morning.

Luncheon was served on sweet china as if catering to a ladies' buffet, rolled to the parlor door on the tea cart by Rosemary, then transferred to Brynn's care at the threshold. There was a small table to be moved to Mrs. Darcy's chair, covered with a snowy cloth, then there was the laying out of the dishes and silverware. Mrs. Darcy always had a glass of buttermilk with her luncheon, followed by a thin glass of wine.

When all was properly arranged, Mrs. Darcy would tell her: "That's fine. You may go have your dinner, now. Thank you." And Brynn would be dismissed to eat and have half an hour to herself.

She could have sat in the kitchen with Rosemary, of course, but instead, she would throw her coat on and whip out into the cold air, feeling like a bird out of prison. It was pure heaven to feel the frigid breeze in her face and breathe in the fresh air as she trotted down the tiny path under the trees to the stable. Mrs. Darcy's gelding would be out in the paddock by this time---apparently another of Rosemary's duties---and she would stop and pat him momentarily before going in to see Angelina.

The stable, like the rest of the place, was quaint and tidy and sweet-smelling and it was no hardship at all for Brynn to sit on a hay bale and eat her lunch. She kept an eagle eye on the time, of course, for Mrs. Darcy took no quarter about punctuality. After the first week, she brought a book with her and by the time it was time to go back, she was actually glad of the heat of the parlor.

"Don't you get yourself too cold out there," Mrs. Darcy warned her. Brynn looked at her in surprise, wondering how she knew where she spent her time. "You'll catch cold out in that barn."

"It's not very cold," she replied. "I don't mind."

"I don't care if you mind or not," the old lady told her. "I mind if you get the sniffles and bring them back to me. I can't abide anyone reading with a cold in the head, either. So mind that you don't catch one."

"Yes, ma'am," Brynn replied.

The reading aloud was the afternoon duty. It was nearly as tiresome as being watched while she cleaned, for the books Mrs. Darcy liked were wordy, otherworldly stories that were nearly incomprehensible to Brynn. She had never been a reader, that was more in Jerusha's line, and, although she liked to write, her compositions were nothing compared to these long, complex volumes.

Sometimes, she was called upon to read the Bible, and that was better, for at least she could understand most of what she was reading and could put some tone into it. But Chaucer, Shakespeare, and Tolstoy were torture. Mrs. Darcy was never charitable in her criticism, and Brynn sometimes wondered which would be the less childish; to burst into tears, or to throw the book across the room.

"She makes me feel like I'm about four years old," she told Boone at home after one of the more vigorously critiqued session. "Now I know why Rosemary doesn't say anything. And why she needed to hire a companion in the first place. Nobody in their right mind would socialize with her for free, not even her own family."

In actual fact, Mrs. Darcy's son and daughter-in-law came by quite often and by the end of her second week, Brynn knew them to be what they were; open, friendly people who resembled the elder Mrs. Darcy not at all. In her mind, she began to call the mother-in-law and daughter-in-law Old Darcy and Young Darcy respectively and to be grateful for the times when there would be a knock on the door and either Young Darcy or Mr. Darcy would come bustling in.

She had met them before, of course, for her parents had known all three for years, but she had never done more than nod and say hello. Now, they meant a friendly word or two and, more importantly, a good extra half-hour of solitude while they visited with Mrs. Darcy in the stuffy parlor.

It also meant that she began to pick up some information about Old Darcy's family.

One afternoon when she had heard Young Darcy leave, she went reluctantly back into the parlor to find Mrs. Darcy looking displeased. That in itself was cause for some caution, for Mrs. Darcy seldom looked anything but displeased, and this transcended even that. She had one hand on her cane, tapping the tip of it against the hearth, the other knotted hand was working at the handkerchief in her lap. Her thin lips pursed themselves irritably.

"Do you want your tea now, Ma'am?" Brynn asked her a little hesitantly.

"It's all about that grandson of mine," Mrs. Darcy replied, as if she were in the middle of a conversation. "I told John that he was too easy on him. The boy is much too smart for his own good and John just went on and let him do whatever he pleased. Was that way with all four of those boys, but that youngest one takes the cake. That's what you young ones say these days, isn't it---takes the cake? That's just about the word for it with Stefan. The other three, they were content to get through school, get their college----**with** my help, if I may say so---and settle in to having families and working like they should. That's to their credit, I suppose, those it's more due to my support and expense getting them through school than their parents efforts. Then, there comes along another, much later than the others. That accounts for John's leniency. Never expected the boy. What are you doing dithering there, Miss Brynnlin?"

"I was just wondering if you would like your tea now, Mrs. Darcy," she replied.

"Well, for heaven's sake, why didn't you say so? And, no, not now. I'm too upset. Ask Rosemary to bring me my tonic. In a double glass, if you please."

Of course Brynn had figured out from the first what Mrs. Darcy's tonic was, and this day she seemed to need it more than usual. Rosemary brought the tumbler full and when Mrs. Darcy had sipped a generous portion, she began again.

"That Stefan," she said. "All that effort they have put into that boy, all that expense at one of the best universities and what does he do? Expelled! That's what he does! Expelled from university for his carousing. Failing his courses, they say. Pranks on the campus. Breaking curfew and not attending classes. So, now he's home. For what purpose is he home? To continue to spend my money? Not on your life, I can assure you of that. I'll have a sandwich now if you please, Brynnlin. It's nearly tea-time, isn't it?"

"Yes, ma'am. Shall I ring for Rosemary or...?"

"Yes, yes, ring for Rosemary. No, on second thought, go back and tell her yourself. 'Tisn't proper for you to be ordering Rosemary around, though she is colored. She's thirty years your elder. You go back and help Rosemary fix my tea."

Of course, she always helped Rosemary fix the tea, although she had learned by hard experience to ask for help whenever she was unsure of exactly how Mrs. Darcy wanted things done. One time of not warming the teapot before putting in the tea leaves was enough. Rosemary never spoke, seldom smiled, but was obliging to her. Brynn got the impression that they were shoulder to shoulder when it came to Mrs. Darcy.

She was very grateful that it was Friday that day. The remainder of the day Mrs. Darcy was harder than ever to please and by the time five o'clock came, Brynn was on a fair way to tearing her hair out---her own hair, not Mrs.

Darcy's. Although that would probably make me feel a hundred percent better, she reflected, as she at last picked up her coat and scarf and skipped out the door.

It was payday, too, and as always, there was an envelope slipped into her coat pocket when she took it off the rack. Apparently, Mrs. Darcy's son or daughter-in-law counted out the bills into the envelope and wrote her name on the outside, for it wasn't Mrs. Darcy's feathery handwriting. She never saw how it got into her coat, and Mrs. Darcy never mentioned it, so she assumed that some arrangements had been made with Rosemary to take care of it all.

She didn't care. She was very glad to be going home, even though it meant that the laundry basket would be overflowing ready for the weekend's washing and she would be up earlier than always to do Saturday's chores.

"I don't care! I don't care!" she was singing happily under her breath as she slipped out the back door. As she went, she reached up with one hand and unwound the bun into which she always twisted her hair, letting it fall down her back.

It was cold out, the sky was low and layered looking and there was a feel of snow in the air. All the better, she thought in delight. Pushing her hair back into its usual tail, she secured it with the heavy clasp and trotted toward the stable. She was so intent on what she was doing, she didn't see the young man near the fence until he spoke.

"Good evening," he said and she skidded to a stop. "Sorry," he added with a laugh in his voice. "Didn't mean to scare you."

"You didn't," Brynn replied. "Well, maybe a little."

He was smiling at her and it made him rather nice looking. It was a cocky sort of smile, though, and although he had her favorite kind of dark, curly hair and blue eyes of which she could tell the color even at the distance of several yards, something about it put her on her guard.

"I am sorry," he said. "I've come to see my grandmother. You must be the companion that my father hired. You must be one of the McKenna girls."

"Yes," she replied.

He looked toward the house a little warily. "I'm not really looking forward to this," he said. "My grandmother's not---well---resting or anything, is she? So that I ought to come back some other time?"

She stifled a smile. "No," she told him. "Actually, she's just had her tea. It may mean she's in a better mood than she's been since your father came by earlier."

He made a pained expression. "Oh," he said. "So, she didn't take the news too good, did she?"

"The news about her grandson being expelled from the university? No, she wasn't too pleased."

The young man shrugged. Without the knowing grin, he was more appealing. "Oh, well. May as well get it over with. Maybe if I go now, she won't have had as much time to think of all the things she wants to say to me."

Brynn wrapped the scarf about her neck and started for the stable, again. "Good luck," she told him.

"Thanks," he said. "Oh, by the way, I'm Steve. Steve Darcy. Which McKenna are you?"

She turned and skipped backward down the path. She didn't want to stop. It was Friday. "I'm Brynn," she told him. "And you're not Steve."

"I'm not?" he asked in surprise. "Who am I then?"

"You're Stefan," she said.

Kevin was concerned about his brother's children.

He told Janine that he spent half his time worrying himself to death about his own children and the other half worrying about Morgan's. He had enough, he figured, to concern himself with, what with the farm and all, without the rest of it.

It had been bad enough when Morgan and Amy's bunch had been right where he could keep tabs on them; when the twins and Sorrel were under his own roof and Brynn over at Kate and Buck's. Now, with them up the hill where he couldn't see them every day---except Jordan---he couldn't tell what was going on with them.

He tried to get a feel for how things were going by casually asking Jordan once in a while, but Jordan was a typical thirteen year old and was not a satisfactory fount of information. If it didn't concern him directly, Jordan wasn't too worried about it. From Jordan, however, Kevin had ascertained that the cooking wasn't the best, that Brynn could be a tyrant when things weren't done to her liking, and that Jordan hadn't had fried chicken for a long time.

Kevin had, of course, told Janine to try to get Jordan to come into New House kitchen and have something to eat from time to time; even have supper and take some leftovers home with him, but Jordan seemed to have acquired some of Brynn's bullheadedness and refused. He never seemed even particularly tempted to do so, didn't look longingly at the handouts that Clay took from the back door after school before going out to help with the farm work, didn't hesitate in his answer or look reluctant when Kevin invited him to stay. But the boy looked thinner to Kevin, his clothes had buttons missing and hung limp and wrinkled on him, his hair sometimes looked unkempt as if no one was reminding him to brush it. Even his hands were dirty, and his fingernails had crescents of black under them. Amy would never have stood for that, he knew. Amy would be appalled.

But, he sighed as he went across the yard toward the paddock, he had made a deal with Brynn and Boone and he would stick with it. It did seem as if Brynn was working out well with Mrs. Darcy, according to the old lady's son, John, at least. John was well pleased with Brynn, although Kevin got the impression that Mrs. Darcy herself had a different opinion. Everyone knew, however, that an angel sent from heaven would not have gotten a stellar review from Mrs. Darcy, so the fact that Brynn was still employed there after a month and a half was testimony in itself.

Boone, too, seemed to have had no problem in staying the course with Carson across the river, even though his place of residency had changed. Kevin hadn't expected anything less from the two of them, actually. He wouldn't have expected anything less from any of Morgan's children, or from his own, either. Work was something that all the children had set before them all their lives.

But he had heard a rumor that there were some worries up at Old House, apart from the expected ones, of course. There was the question of Jerusha's schooling come fall. Kevin knew that Morgan had planned on her going to Virginia and had had some money put away for that purpose, but the doctor bills during their last illness and the burials had drained that fund. Word around was that Brynn still planned on Jerusha going but how that was to be accomplished, no one much knew. Kevin also was well aware, as he hoped Boone and Brynn were, that the note on the well would be coming due pretty soon.

He had thought that he should sit the two of them down and remind them of that, maybe work out a plan or a budget with their finances, but then had discarded the idea. After Morgan's death, he had taken Boone to the bank and they had opened the books and gone over it all. Boone knew where to look to find out what he needed to know.

Boone hadn't liked being in that bank, hadn't liked Kevin being there and hadn't liked the whole idea of the business end of Old House, Kevin could tell. Brynn, too wouldn't appreciate her uncle butting in, reminding them of the things that they should already know. She and Boone were grown, after all. At least Boone was. Anyway, they swore all up and down that they were.

And if they did mess up the finances, what was the worst that could happen, anyway? They would lose Old House, the children would come back down to live with Kevin and Janine and Brynn would be back at Kate's. Which, to everybody's mind except their own, was where they should all be anyway. So, Kevin decided he would let the chips fall where they may. If they wanted to handle it, they could handle it.

Taylor, the hired man, came strolling up the hill inside the paddock, swinging a lead. The two or three horses inside the fence moved away from him as he came. Seeing Kevin, he altered his path and met him at the fence. Taylor had a craggy, weathered face which seemed to never be surprised at anything life could show him. He leaned on the top rail and spat a stream of tobacco juice to the ground before asking:

"What's on this morning, Boss?"

Kevin sighed. He didn't know why he should be so all-fired set on all this; so much so that he would take part of a Saturday to see about it. Still…

"I'm going to take a walk up the hill for a bit," he replied.

Taylor nodded, chewing pensively. "Go see the younguns?" he asked.

"Yes, I guess I'll go on and see about this now," he told him. "Do me a favor---take a count of the Old House cattle, would you? Make sure it tallies with the books. They're probably scattered all through the herd. Take Buck if you want to. Tell him I told him too. I'd like it done by this evening."

The tall thin man nodded again. "Will do," he replied. "Want we should cut them out and put them in the lower pasture?"

Kevin considered, then said: "No, I don't think so. Just find out for sure if we've lost any."

Old House was pandemonium. He had figured that it would be, it being the one morning a week that Brynn and Boone had off. Sunday didn't count, of course, for Sunday really wasn't an off day. By the look of things, Saturday wasn't, either. Kevin stood just inside the door to the kitchen and looked at it all.

There was the big wash tub full of steaming water in the middle of the floor, water boiling on the stove for the rinse and heaps of dirty clothes all around. Jerusha and Brynn were standing, facing each other, each with their hands on their hips, each with their chins stuck out, both yelling as loud as they could get, so loud in fact that neither they nor anyone else realized that Kevin was there.

Sorrel was at the dishpan, washing dishes with one hand and wiping her eyes with the other; Boone was peering into the pantry with a pencil and paper in his hand, making lists; Jordan was eating cold oatmeal out of the pot. The only one who seemed aware of another person in the room was Tommycat who made a dash for the outside before Kevin managed to close the door.

"I am not going to do it!" Jerusha was screaming. "You can't make me! You're not Mama and you can't make me!"

"Oh yes I can make you, you little monster!" Brynn yelled back at her. "That's your room and it smells like something died in there and you are going to sweep and mop that floor before you go anywhere!"

"I'm going with Boone!" Jerusha stated flatly, stamping her foot emphatically. "It's my turn to go to market and I'm going. You can't stop me!"

"Boone won't take you," Brynn told her. "If you don't do your chores, you don't go anywhere, that's the rule!"

"That's not my chore! My chore was to strip the beds and tidy my side of the room and I did that. Sweeping and mopping ain't my chore! Make Sorrel do it."

"It ain't **my** chore," Sorrel put in mildly, wiping her nose on her sleeve.

"So I suppose it's **my** chore just like everything else in the damn place!" Brynn said.

"Yes!" Jerusha said. "You think it stinks so bad, you clean in there. I'm going with Brother!"

"You are not going with Boone if that's not done!" Brynn began again.

Jordan passed by the door, pot and spoon in hand, to go sit at the table. "Hey, Uncle Kevin," he said.

"Good morning," Kevin replied.

"Is it?" the boy said.

Boone looked over from his position at the pantry. "Oh, hello," he said under cover of the girls' raised voices.

"Morning, Boone."

"Hey, Uncle," Sorrel said from the sink.

"Morning, Sorrel."

"Boone will take me whether you want me to go or not!" Jerusha was continuing. "You ain't the boss of him!"

"You want to bet!"

Boone turned his head and gave one of his father's piercing whistles between his teeth, the kind you didn't want to be standing next to. Kevin winced a little. Both girls stopped in midair and looked toward them. Boone jerked his thumb in Kevin's direction.

"Oh," Brynn said. "Hello."

"Uncle Kevin," Jerusha said. "Do I got to do everything Brynn says?"

Kevin looked from one set of brown eyes to the other. "Well, I think you pretty much do," he replied. "After all, she's earning a good part of the money around here."

"She sits at the head of the table," Sorrel put in quietly.

"Oh, I hate all of y'all!" Jerusha said, her fists balled up. "You're all a bunch of...!" She struggled to find the word, then blew a vicious raspberry to compensate and slammed up the stairs.

There was a moment of silence, then Brynn said: "Boone, you need to just go on to town."

"I will."

"Can I go if Rue ain't?" Sorrel asked.

"No," both Brynn and Boone told her.

"You want some coffee, Kev?" Brynn asked him, wiping back damp tendrils of hair from her forehead.

"Well..," he said.

"I made it," Boone told him in an aside.

"Sounds good," Kevin replied, giving his niece one of his smiles. "If Boone made it." Brynn was enough like her mother that she couldn't help smiling back when he did.

"I won't be insulted at that," she said. "Boone, if you're going…"

"Actually," her uncle said. "Before you go, I need to talk to the two of you about something. It won't take long," he added at their faces. "It's not earth shaking, just business."

When Brynn had poured his coffee and they were sitting at the table, Jordan still scraping the oatmeal pot, Kevin said to them: "You know that your Daddy put Old House cattle in with New House, yes? And that some were sold at auction last fall."

"I thought all of them had been sold," Boone said. "And paid off the bills and all that."

Kevin was unfolding the paper out of his pocket and putting his reading glasses on. "Well, not all were sold," he replied. "I've got an approximate count here and also what the last lot brought per head in November," he slid the paper around so they could read it. "Also what was paid out of that, for doctor bills and such---that's this here. Taylor's down doing a count this morning on the head that are left, just to make sure of where we are. I kept some back, just in case. And I know that your Daddy and Mama had wanted Rue to go off to school, and that there are some other things that may come up, so I just wanted to let you know what cattle are down at my place with your brand on them, in case you want to sell some next fall."

He looked at both of them, at the surprise on their faces. They were staring at the paper. "There's probably a few heifers in calf," he added. "You'll need to decide if you want to keep some back for breeding or sell them all off. It's up to you, of course. Won't have to decide till after the summer. Auction is in September."

Jordan craned his neck to see the figures. Sorrel came from the sink and looked over Brynn's shoulder, wiping her hands on her apron. Kevin had thought maybe it would have been best to just talk to Boone, or maybe Boone and Brynn alone, but it seemed that, since they had moved up to Old House, the whole bunch of them wanted to be on every decision. He supposed that made sense, really. The twins and Sorrel were still so young, though.

"Wow," Jordan said. "We got money."

"Well, we ain't got it yet," Brynn told him.

"Yes, and it'll go pretty quick on train fare for Rue and clothes she'll need and God knows what all," Boone put in. "Not to mention taxes put back for next year."

"When are taxes due?" Sorrel asked.

"November, right Kevin?"

"Yes," he agreed.

"Oh, that's ages from now," Sorrel said.

"No, it ain't," Boone told her. "It's just around the corner."

"Is not. Ain't even March yet."

"Well, a lot can happen between here and then."

"So, we're not sure how many head we have yet?" Brynn broke in.

Kevin pushed his glasses up on his nose. "Not yet. We'll know by this afternoon if you want to run down and find out."

"It is nice to think we have something out there to fall back on," Brynn said. She smiled at him. "Did Daddy tell you to keep some back and not sell them all?"

"No, I just couldn't bring myself to do it. I thought maybe having a few irons in the fire wouldn't be amiss."

"Thank you," she told him.

They talked awhile longer and then, before he left, Kevin went up to see Jerusha. There had been no sound from upstairs while the conference had been going on, and as he went down the short hall and knocked on the door of the room she shared with Sorrel, it was so quiet, he wondered if she had made her escape when they were occupied. However, at his knock, there was a muffled:

"Go away!"

"Rue, it's me," Kevin said and the next moment, the door was opened and he braced himself as she threw herself into his arms.

"Oh, Uncle Kevin, can you see how hateful they all are!" the girl burst out. "Brynn is the worst one and Boone won't do anything to make her quit and Jordan is meaner than anything!"

"I didn't see that Jordan was doing anything much," he replied. "Here, wipe your nose," he added, handing her his handkerchief. "You done what you were supposed to do? You cleaned your room?"

"My room **was** clean," she said, walking to the middle of the floor and spreading her hands. "Look. See?"

He followed her into the room and surveyed it, then sniffed appraisingly. "Well, it may **look** that way, but she's right about the smell," he replied.

It was a typical room that two girls shared with quilts spread over the two beds, flowered curtains hung that Amy had taken such care picking out, and a few good pictures framed on the walls. There was a book or two dropped on the floor, and he was sure that his wife would think that the dust clinging to the corners was deplorable, but all in all, considering, it wasn't too bad. But there was a definite aroma about the place.

"Rue," he said. "Have you swept under the beds?"

"Well," she replied slowly. "Not recently."

"Well, I think maybe we best take a look under there," he took hold of the foot-rail and pulled the bed out from the wall. "Ah," he said. "I think we found it."

"What?" Jerusha asked. "What did we find?"

"The smell," he told her and, bending, picked up the dead mouse by the tail. "Good grief, girl, how can you sleep in a room that smells like this?"

Jerusha gave a mild shriek and leaped to the bed. "Ooo, yuk, Uncle!" she said, getting as far from it as she could without climbing up the wall. "It's not---is it? Is it---dead?"

"Definitely," he told her, heading for the window and shoving up the sash with one hand. "For quite awhile." He tossed the corpse out into the bushes below. "I suggest you leave the window open for a bit and close the door so you don't freeze out the rest of the house. Heaven's to Betsy, girlie," he said. "No wonder your sister was having a fit. I'd have been having one, too."

Jerusha climbed down off the bed with a flounce. "Well, she's always like that. If it's not about one thing, it's another."

He took a look at her. "And you don't mind getting her that way, either, do you?"

She shrugged.

"What's the matter, Rue?" he said kindly. "Things kind of tough on you?"

She looked up at him sideways and there were some real tears there. "I miss my Daddy," she said succinctly.

He sighed and pulled her back into his arms. "I know you do, baby," he told her. "I do, too." He patted her back a minute. "But, your sister and brother Boone do too, you know. And they're trying to do the best they can." She mumbled something indistinguishable. "You're just going to have to be patient with each other, that's all. And everybody has to do their part."

"It was my turn to go to town," she said from his shirt front.

"Well, Boone's not gone yet, I don't think," he said. "Maybe you can catch him. Now that the smelly thing is out."

When he left, Brynn was washing a stack of laundry that made Kevin wonder how she would ever get through it all, Jerusha was off to the market with her brother, and the others were helping put the kitchen dishes to rights. They all were looking a bit happier, he was glad to see. Just taking a little of the worry off of them set his mind more at rest.

Now if the other problem in his life could be relieved that easily, he thought as, heading down the hill toward New House, he saw Adam's horse outside his back door.

He shouldn't be thinking of his second son as a problem, he told himself, riding at a slow gait down the hill toward home. The sight of Adam's horse didn't make him hurry. He was sure he was alone, which was a relief, although if he brought Gideon, that would make Kevin's day. But at least he hadn't brought Bethy.

Kevin had stopped trying to be comfortable with Adam's wife some time ago. Just as, he believed, Adam had. The problem, he knew, wasn't due to Bethy completely, it was the marriage in general. Everybody knew that the marriage wasn't going well. Everybody knew, just as everybody knew why. The whole thing had been a mistake from the beginning, even though Gideon had been the happy outcome. But Gideon couldn't be expected to hold things together when everything else was so completely falling apart.

Adam was in the kitchen with Janny and one look at his face made Kevin's heart sink. One look at Janine's face, and the fact that Adam was alone without his son, made him brace himself for the worst. The boy was sitting at the kitchen table and when Kevin came in, he said without preamble:

"Bethy went back to Duggansville, Pa. She took Gid and left sometime yesterday. They were gone when I got home from work. Says it's for an 'extended visit'. Whatever that means."

Kevin flipped his hat onto the rack and sighed. "Just like that? No word to you at all?"

"Well, she left me a note," Adam replied. "I guess you could say that was word." He pulled out the folded paper and handed it to his father, who didn't look at it. "She says she's homesick and misses her mama and she'll write to say when she'll be coming back."

"Did the two of you have a fight again?"

He gave a short laugh. "When don't we have a fight? But, no, nothing unusual." He fingered the cup between his hands. "Didn't even let me say good-bye to my own son."

Kevin looked across at Janine. She said nothing, but she was seething, he could tell. He went and sat near him, clapping him on the shoulder. "So what are you going to do?" he asked.

"I don't know. I wrote her mama this morning, asking her to get Bethy to write as soon as she gets there. Then sent another to Bethy herself at her parents'. I don't know what else the hell to do. I got a job here. I ain't going running after her begging her to come home."

There was the other question, of course. The bigger question of whether they would stay married or not even if she did come home. No one in the family as far back as anyone could remember had ever been divorced. Kevin didn't think he had ever known anybody outside of the family who was for that matter. And, of course, there was the Brynn factor. Kevin always thought of it as the Brynn factor. The reason that Adam had gone to Duggansville that year in the first place had be because of his feelings for Brynn. And Kevin knew, although nothing had been said to him, that Adam's feelings hadn't changed.

"On the other hand," Adam said after a moment. "I ain't going to sit waiting here and not see him for months at a time. He's so little, if he don't see me every day, he'll forget about me. Or as good as---start wondering what happened to me, think I don't care about him. Not to mention what she'll be telling him. So, what am I supposed to do then?"

"First off," Janine told him briskly. "You need a good breakfast. And don't tell me you've had one already; I know you haven't cooked anything for yourself."

"Ma, I'm not hungry."

"That's not the point," she replied rather cryptically. "You need to eat." She set down the plate before him and then a full cup of coffee. "You can't think straight on an empty stomach."

Kevin poured a cup for himself and they sat and talked for awhile. Kevin was glad to see that the boy seemed a bit happier after he ate, even smiling from time to time. At length, he got up, kissed his mother and said he had to be going.

"Think I'll swing up to Old House for a bit," he said. Then, in an altered tone, he added: "Don't worry, Mother, I'll try to restrain myself and not jump into bed with Brynnie while I'm there."

As he left out the back door, Kevin said to her in a low voice: "Well, that's exactly what you were thinking."

Brynn had hung out the first load of laundry when she saw Adam coming up the hill on his horse from New House. She paused, the empty basket on her hip, thinking with a pang that there were innumerable horses and riders coming and going between one house and another on any given day, but only Adam caught and held her attention.

She sighed, watching the tall young man with the glossy black hair stop down at the fence and dismount, swinging down with that particular grace that attracted so many. She wished she didn't feel like she did.

"Good morning," he said, walking up the hill to her.

"Hello," she replied.

She didn't know how she appealed to him, Adam knew. She always had that look to her; that shy look, the half-averted face, the glance from under the heavy lashes when she thought he wasn't watching. He always watched her, however.

He had watched her all her life, in one way or another. For most of the time, she had been just one of the bunch of cousins that were pests in the extreme; always wanting to come along with him and Boone, always getting in the way. Even then, however, she had been too cute to be cruel to or to snub so completely that she left them alone. He had been her defender against Boone's more substantial cold shoulder, a fact that Brynn had figured out immediately and played to her advantage.

He had always had a soft spot for her. When it had turned into something more, she had leaped into that, too with a free-fall abandon. And his marriage had hurt her mightily. Now, she didn't think he cared at all; she had decided that he never had, he knew. He had never dissuaded her from that opinion. It had been best that she thought that. But now...

"Where is everybody?" he asked her.

She had her hair down, not done up in that bun that she wore every day now that she was working. She had it pulled back and in its heavy clasp, the wind catching it into hovering wisps about her head. It was cold out, despite the sunshine; she wore a short coat over trousers, a scarf tucked inside the collar, gloves on her hands with the fingers out. The cold brought color to her olive complexion, the muted light glinted off her locket. "They're around," she replied.

"Boone and Rue went to town, Sorrel's upstairs, Jimbo---I don't know. Around."

"Glad to have a day off?" he asked.

Then she smiled, as he had hoped that she would. "Oh, yes," she said with conviction.

"How's old lady Darcy treating you?"

"Well, it's a job," she replied. "It's money. If she made me lie down and walked on me, I guess I couldn't complain. And it's not too bad, I guess."

"I hear her grandson's back in town," he said. "Back from college."

"Back permanently, so he says," she replied. "He got kicked out or something."

"You've seen him then?"

"Yes, once."

"I remember him some from school," he said, taking off his hat so the wind could blow through his hair. "He was a few years back from me and Boone, I think. Bout your age?"

She shrugged. "I don't know. I think he went to prep school somewhere, so Old Darcy---I mean Mrs. Darcy says."

" 'Old Darcy'?" he grinned. "Is that what you call her?"

"When nobody's listening who would care."

There was a pause. He turned his hat in his hands, looking at it, then decided that there was no nice way to say it. "Bethy's left town," he told her, not looking to see her reaction. "Just came by to tell you."

"Left?" she repeated.

"Yesterday while I was at work, apparently. Took the train, her and Gid. Went back to her mama. She says for a visit." He could hear the clipped curt tone in his own voice. "Came home and they were gone."

"Oh, Adam," she said. "Well, I guess she would want to go back for a visit." He looked at her then, and saw that there was real concern in the brown eyes. He wasn't close enough to see the gold in them, but he knew it was there.

"That's a nice way to put it. If a visit is what she really has in mind."

"What else would she be doing, then?"

"I thought everybody knew how things were with us," he said. "Don't act like you don't know, too."

"Oh," she said, and looked uncomfortable.

She was really very young, he thought then. There were times since her parents died that Brynn had seemed grown and capable and no nonsense. It was only when the two of them were alone together that she still showed that she was not yet out of her teens. And the two of them being alone was a rare thing.

"What will you do now?" she asked after a moment.

"That's what everyone keeps asking," he said. "That's what I keep asking myself. I don't know yet." His gaze wandered to the old house with the bay windows curving, then to the windy sky, then back to her. "I don't want to leave," he added.

"I don't want you to, either," she replied, right to him.

"I guess I shouldn't have married her," he said. "I shouldn't have done a lot of things. But…"

She dropped her gaze then. "You went to Duggansville in the first place because of me," she said.

"I went because of the way I felt about you," he corrected her. "That wasn't your fault. Anyway," he said. "What's done is done. And my son is caught in the middle of it. So, what I need to figure out now is what's best for Gideon, all in all. He's got to come first in all this."

"Yes," she said.

What he really wanted to do was go to her and hold her, there in the wind. And what he wanted to do was irrelevant, so instead he told her: "Well, I got to go. I just wanted to come by and tell you."

"All right," she said and her voice was thin.

When he was gone, Brynn was able to cry a little while she went on scrubbing the laundry on the washboard without anybody noticing. If Boone had been there, he would have noticed, but Boone didn't get back with the groceries until she was hanging the second load on the line. And by that time, she had gotten herself in hand again.

-4-

Jackson Flynn had gotten back to Dooley and had heard that the McKenna children were living in Old House on their own, but he hadn't bothered to go out to see them.

He had actually seen the younger ones outside the schoolhouse a time or two at recess, and had seen sundry other McKennas in town, but still he didn't approach any of them. It was only when he happened to run across Stephen Darcy outside the feed and seed that he even acknowledged his curiosity about how they were doing. And that was only because Steve knew him too well.

Steve Darcy was one of those people who could relate to just about everybody, at least if the person was male. He related to females quite well, too, but in a different way. He talked openly to anyone, but he was a man's man, even if he was not quite to his nineteenth birthday.

Jackson found it strange that a kid nine years his junior was the one that he picked as the closest thing he had to a friend in Dooley, but he did. Of course, Brynn McKenna, the one girl that he couldn't get out of his mind was ten years his junior, so maybe there was a pattern. Maybe I'm just a kid at heart, he thought ruefully, as he crossed the street at Stephen's wave.

"Well, what the hell wind blew you into town?" he asked the younger man, stepping up onto the sidewalk and shaking his hand.

Stephen grinned, glad to see him. He liked talking to Flynn. He didn't expect anything from him. "You mean you haven't heard?" he asked. "You must be the only person in town that my parents haven't complained to."

"I did hear something about you coming home for an 'extended' visit," Jackson replied. "I figured that meant that that high-priced school of yours didn't want you any more."

"Pretty much," Stephen said. "Actually, I got kicked out and I won't bore you with the details."

Jackson always attracted a certain amount of attention, Stephen reflected as two young ladies passed by and gave him a second look. He dressed so like a mountain man with his fringed jacket, stained by weather, belted at the waist, and his fringed buckskin boots to the knee. All out of fashion, and mysteriously dangerous. The fact that he was tall, spare, and had dark hair and gray eyes didn't hurt, either. Stephen didn't mind being seen with him.

"So what are you going to do now?" he asked Stephen. "Now that your college education is over. I presume it is over, is it?"

"As far as I'm concerned, it is," he replied. "And as far as my grandmother's donations to the college fund, that's over too, and my folks can't afford it, even if my father wanted to---which he doesn't----so I guess that's it. Fine with me. You know what I always wanted to do, anyway."

"You're not still on that, are you?" Jackson asked. "You don't still want to start that newspaper, do you?"

"Well, I went to college to study journalism so I could, but in this town you don't have to have a degree to start up something. Town needs a newspaper, I need a job; why not?"

"Why not just go to work with you father like everybody else does around here?"

"In the train station? No thanks. If I'm going to work at anything, it'll be something I want to do. And, I guess I **do** have to work, so..." he shrugged.

"Where're you going to set up this enterprise, anyway?" Jackson asked in amusement. "I mean, you do have to have someplace to set up shop, don't you? Printing press, paper, things like that?"

Stephen rocked on his heels, his hands in his pockets. He looked pleased with himself. "As a matter of fact," he replied. "Well, come on. Let's walk. I'll show you what I've been thinking about."

The two started down the board sidewalk. It was a fine day for February; cold but not too cold, with enough bite to the air to sting the lungs, but warm in the sunshine around a sheltered corner. The sky was blazing blue, painted with mare's tails. The shopkeepers who pretended to know said that they were due a snow in the next few days. It had been a quiet winter in the hills so far; they were due a good dose of winter weather.

The two men hadn't gone ten yards when their progress was blocked by the sudden appearance of a customer coming hurriedly out of Habersham's Merchantile. Both nearly plowed over her; both actually collided with her, and both begged her pardon and stepped back, touching their hats. She stumbled, Jackson caught her arm to steady her, and when she turned toward them, they saw who it was. It was Brynn McKenna.

She was out of breath, carrying a market basket, and her words came out frothy in the cold air. "Oh, good grief," she said and her smile was for both of them. "I'm so sorry. I'm not looking where I'm going today."

"Our fault," Jackson said.

"That's all right," Stephen added.

"It was definitely not your fault," she said, smoothing her hair with one hand. "I've been rushing with myself all day." She took a breath and added: "Hello."

They were right in the way of anyone trying to get in or out. Jackson took her elbow and maneuvered her aside from two ladies passing. The girl was in her work getup, Stephen saw. Her hair was in its bun at the back of her head, she had on the same nothing-color dress he had seen her in before, with her scarlet-trimmed brown knit hat and brown gloves. Nothing to catch anybody's attention.

"You doing errands for my grandmother?" Stephen asked her.

"Yes," she patted the basket comfortably. "Just a few things. Too few to make it worth Rosemary coming all the way into town, but I don't mind."

"I'll bet," he grinned. "I wouldn't mind anything that got me out of that house, either."

"The run is good for me," she replied. "Hello, Jackson," she said to him.

"Miss McKenna," he said. "I heard you were working now. How are things going up at Old House?"

"Well," she said. "As well as you would expect with a bunch of children trying to run it. But, we're managing. We've---umm—we've missed you. Jordan's been wondering when you'd get back in town. You've been trapping, I suppose."

"Yes," he told her. "Tell Jimbo I'll be out his way pretty soon."

"He'll be glad to see you," she said. "Maybe you could get out his way and eat supper sometime. That is, if you're brave enough. I can't guarantee how it'll be. My sisters are the cooks these days."

"I'll chance it," he told her, smiling.

"Can I come?" Stephen asked. Jackson gave him a look and Stephen responded with a surprised one of his own.

Brynn laughed. "I don't know if we're up to a dinner party quite yet," she said.

"Yes, and I've got dibs, so tough luck," Jackson told him easily.

"Oh, all right, I'll wait till spring," Stephen said. "But tell your sisters I like my dinners the three or four course kind."

She started on her way down the side walk and they made way for her, pulling their hat brims again. "I think you may be out of luck in that case," she told him. She waved her fingers to them both and they both were left standing, looking after her in silence.

"Well," Stephen said. He sighed and realized that Jackson had done the same.

"Yes, well," Jackson agreed as they started off again. "When did you meet Rebecca?"

"Who?"

"Brynn. Her first name's Rebecca. When did you meet her?"

"I knew her in school," Stephen said. "But not for long, since I went away to prep school. Saw her awhile back at my grandmother's when I got home. And see here," he added as they stepped down off the sidewalk and crossed the side street before the sheriff's office. "Why do you get to go eat supper over at her house and I don't?"

"Who says you don't?"

"I could've shaved with the look you gave me. You go over there a lot, do you?"

"I don't go anywhere in this town a lot."

"Ah, but you would like to go over there a lot, wouldn't you? That's what I thought. Can't get away with anything with me, Flynn. I'm a reporter, you know."

"Morning, boys," the sheriff said as they passed. Karl Barnes had been duly elected sheriff for a couple of years now. He was single, broad-shouldered and no-nonsense and word was that he swung a heavy billy club. He had a keen eye and a perpetual amused expression, even when arresting a perpetrator.

They both said good-morning and when they had gotten out of ear-shot, Jackson said: "I ain't trying to 'get away' with anything anyway. I took her little brother hunting once or twice, that's all. He's a good kid."

"And his older sister ain't too bad, either."

"Anybody with half an eye knows that," he agreed. "Where're we going, anyway?"

The building where Stephen stopped wasn't big, but it had been a store and had a big store-front window with a For Sale or Rent sign on it and Stephen took Jackson inside as if he was the proprietor already. The owner had given him key, he told Jackson. He knew Stephen's family and had been trying to rent the place so long, he was glad to accommodate. Jackson stepped down the one low step into the big, empty room and looked at it.

"Not bad," he allowed, turning slowly. There was a fair-sized main room, a miniscule lean-to could be seen at the back and a twisting staircase came down from above. "Sure this is big enough for what you want to do?"

Stephen ran one hand over the window sill and fingered the dust. "I think what we'll do is, put the printing press in the window here. Let the folks see how we do things. Let them see it in operation. That'll free up the rest of the room for desk, some storage. Back room with a stove in it. We could move the stove out here for heat, coffee pot. Upstairs is big enough for living space. So I don't have to keep living at my folks'. There's one catch, though," he added.

Jackson stopped turning and looked at him. "What's that?"

"There's a fellow living in the back room," Stephen said. "He's not here much, but he comes with the place."

"Comes with it?"

"Yes, the owner says that he worked for him for a bunch of years, got no family or nothing and he made a deal that when the place gets sold or whatever, he gets to stay."

"No wonder it's not moving," Jackson said.

"He's not a bad sort," Stephen said. "Not so very old, but a little cranky. Not the kind you'd want to have if it was a dress-shop, you know. But, I figure we can live with him."

"Who's this 'we' you keep talking about?"

"Well," Stephen said. "Whoever works with me, you know. And whoever I can get as an investor. To put up capitol."

" Capitol," Jackson repeated.

"Yes, you see," Stephen said. "it's this way. I get an investor to put up the cash for what I need to get started, then the investor owns part of the newspaper. Shares profits. When there are any, that is."

"**If** there are any," Jackson said, with emphasis.

"Yeah, all right, if."

"Where are you planning on finding this deep-pockets?"

Stephen tried to look casual. "Well, word is that you do a pretty good business trapping."

"Word is, is it."

"And it would turn a profit, I guarantee."

"How do you do that? Guarantee it?"

"Think about it, Jack. There's no newspaper any closer than Hampton Cross and Weaversville. Folks around here aren't interested in stuff that happens there. At least, they would be more interested in news about what's happening right here in their home town. News about people they know."

"Yes, except nothing ever happens around here."

"You'd be surprised, I bet. **I'd** be surprised, come to think of it. After all, this is the county seat. There's got to be law news, court cases, even if they are from out of town, it's happening here. And folks like their picture in the paper. I already got a camera. I'd report on every sewing circle and ladies' missionary circle election---with photos---and they'd buy them right up. And besides," he added. "You having an investment business, looks real good to some folks. Makes a respectable resume."

"A what? A resume? For who?"

"For you."

"What do I need a resume for?" Jackson demanded.

"Well," Stephen said. "Just in case you would, say, want to get in good with some girl's family or other, you could point to more than just a trap line as a means of support."

"Some girl meaning Rebecca, I suppose."

"Well, it's written all over you, you know," Stephen told him. "Come on, Jack. Give it some thought, anyway."

"What, marrying Brynn McKenna or the paper?"

"The newspaper first. Then, who knows? And if you make an investment in the paper, I'll make myself scarce with Brynn and give you a fighting chance."

Jackson looked at him. "Thanks." He took a long look about the place, at the dust and cobwebs and the foggy window. "What you planning on calling this newspaper, anyway?"

Stephen put his hands in his pockets and rocked expansively. "I was thinking about 'The Dooley Courier'. What do you think?"

Jackson went with Stephen Darcy to the bank and handed over a tidy sum as Stephen opened an account. Stephen's father signed the papers, since Stephen was under age, but by the end of the week, word around was that the old store on the corner near the sheriff's office was rented and that there was a newspaper coming to town. The town was moving up, people began to say. First the railroad sending a line down to link up over at Hampton Cross, and now a newspaper. Before you knew it, they'd be needing a deputy to help out Sheriff Barnes.

Stephen's grandmother got the news about her grandson's business venture second hand and it was enough to send her ringing for her tonic. Brynn tried to stay out of her way that afternoon and managed to keep the fact that she knew Stephen from her, holding her breath that Young Darcy or her husband might spill the beans.

"It's all right, Mother Darcy," Young Darcy kept telling her when she came to visit. "It's something Steve's always wanted to do. Start a newspaper. That's why he was studying journalism, don't you know?"

"Yes, I do know," Mrs. Darcy retorted. "What he's always wanted to do, my hind leg. What he's always wanted to do was raise the most Cain with the least work, that's what he always wanted to do. And he has succeeded, as usual. Newspaper!"

Young Darcy stayed rather longer than usual, for her mother-in-law had quite a bit to get off her mind. Fortunately, Mrs. Darcy's son was also there, so Young Darcy was able to slip away on some pretence to the kitchen while her husband was talking in the parlor. Brynn was having a quiet cup of tea while Rosemary was making biscuit, and she jumped up hurriedly as Young Darcy came in.

"Oh, don't mind me, dear," the lady told her, pushing back some straggling hair off her forehead. "You sit and have your tea. Hello, Rosemary. How are you?"

Rosemary nodded to her with her quiet smile and went back to her mixing bowl.

"My, it's warm in that parlor," Young Darcy said. "I just came to get a glass of water. Brynn, dear, how is your family? How is Kevin McKenna? And his dear wife?"

"They're very well, thank you, ma'am," Brynn told her. "Would you like me to get your water for you, Mrs. Darcy?"

Stephen's mother was already at the big pump. Mildred Darcy had been born and raised in Dempster County, the daughter of a farmer, and she wielded the pump handle with a strong arm. "Good gracious, no," she replied. "You just sit tight. You don't have to wait on me." She sent water splashing into the glass she held, drank deeply, and then turned a sharp eye on the girl at the end of the room.

"Tell me, Miss Brynn," she said. "How do you like working here so far?"

Brynn had been in the middle of a swallow, and her question almost sent it down the wrong way. She recovered nicely, however, and caught a glimpse of a smile from Rosemary. "I like it fine, ma'am," she replied. "Mrs. Darcy and I get along all right."

The older lady nodded. "Well, I must say, you've lasted longer than I would have thought you would. And my mother-in-law seems quite satisfied with your performance. How long have you worked, now? A month or more, hasn't it? Well, seems that maybe a bit of a raise may be in order."

Brynn stared. "Ma'am?"

"You know that my husband pays your wages, don't you? His mother wouldn't have paid near enough, so he has taken it on. And we're grateful for anyone who can, well, who does so well with his mother. And Rosemary reports that you're prompt and thorough and reliable---I think it's time for a bit of a bonus. I'll speak to my husband about it."

So, that Friday, Brynn found two extra bills in her envelope and was in such a good mood, she actually sent word by Boone and Sorrel when they went to market the next day, that Jackson was invited to supper the next evening.

"You sure?" Boone asked as he made out the list and Brynn stood tying Sorrel's wool hat under her chin.

She looked at him. "What do you mean am I sure?"

"Well, what are you going to cook for him?"

"I don't know. Chicken and dumplings. We got plenty of flour."

"Chicken and dumplings!" Jordan echoed. "Hot damn!"

Brynn turned on him, aghast. "Jimbo, stop that cussing!"

"You made a mess of it last time," Boone reminded, still writing. He was in the pantry, looking over the canned goods.

"Well, I've learned something since then," she informed him. "Anyway, it's just Jackson. What do you care what he eats? Or if he thinks it's any good when he does eat it?"

"Seems like you'd care," her brother said. "But it's no skin off my nose. You ready, Shrimp?"

"Where're your gloves?" Brynn asked her. "Are these the only ones you have? They've got holes all in them."

"It's all right, Sister," Sorrel replied, pulling them on. Nearly every finger was torn.

Brynn sighed. "I've just got to get some time to darn some things," she muttered. "If Janine sees that, she'll have a fit. Jordan," she added. "Carry the laundry basket out to the line for me, would you? It's stinking heavy."

"I'm going out," Jordan told her.

"Not before your room's clean and the laundry basket is out at the line. Where's Rue?"

"She's cleaning her room," Sorrel said, following Boone out the door.

"A likely story," Brynn began poking clothes into the big rinse pot on the stove with the wooden stick. "Jimbo—the basket."

The day actually went better than most, she reflected later that afternoon as the chicken and dumplings were bubbling on the stove. It was clear and cold and even so, in the sunshine, the clothes dried on the line and the big blocks of yellow through the bank of windows warmed the kitchen.

The smell of supper cooking was nearly like home, she thought. Strange to feel that way, since she had lived at Old House so long and it had been home from the very first; but now without her parents, it hadn't been home at all. The smell of supper made it more so.

She had gotten the laundry done, and that fact did her heart good. It wasn't dampened for the ironing, in fact, it was piled unceremoniously in the basket from the line and would probably stay that way until she got to it, but at least it was clean and dry, and that was close to miraculous. If she could keep Tommycat from sleeping in it, so much the better.

The floor was swept, the table wiped down and the cloth was spread, ready to be set and, contrary to her usual behavior, Jerusha had actually done a passable job dusting the front room. Now, she thought, if I could just get myself presentable, I might just have a good time tonight.

As she passed the downstairs bedroom, she caught a glimpse of herself in the mirror over the dresser. She had been loath to even go into the room which her parents had shared, but this day, without thinking about it, she went to the dresser and tried to look at herself objectively. Well, she thought, I suppose not too bad. Not for somebody who's supposed to be the head of a houseful of children and not turned eighteen yet.

Her dark hair was untidy; she undid the clip and shook it down, running her fingers through to smooth it. It was thick and straight as Boone's, hanging nearly to her waist. She wished she was more willowy, like Katie, but she was shorter and broader through the shoulders, was too busty for her liking and only her constant riding kept her bottom in control. Oh, well, she decided. After all, it was only Jackson. Even though she and everyone else knew how he felt about her, she still felt like he was a member of the family, not a suitor.

Almost without realizing what she was doing, she picked up the brush that lay on the dresser, and began to scrub at her hair. In an instant, however, she remembered whose brush it was and stopped with it still against her head. She saw, in just that moment, her mother sitting here in her nightgown as she would be whenever Brynn would tap at their door for a bedtime consult or confession.

She would tap at their door, Amy would call come in, and there she would be, turning toward the door with an expression of half-expectancy, half-apprehension, this same brush in her hand, the very locket Brynn now wore would be hanging about her neck. Her hair was as long as Brynn's own, but blonde and streaked and curling about her face. Her Daddy would already be in bed with his book, a look of bemused annoyance on his face, wondering what it would be this time.

She paused only a moment, then went on brushing, taking a certain comfort in the pull and catch through the tangles. This used to be her brush, she thought firmly, but it isn't now.

"You know," Boone said at supper that night. "This ain't half bad, Bernie."

"Thanks," she replied, dryly.

Jackson was helping himself to seconds and Jordan was hovering for the spoon.

"You shoulda been here when she tried to make scrambled eggs the first time," Jerusha said.

"It was awful," Sorrel put in.

"It was worse than awful," Jerusha said. "And she wasted a whole dozen eggs."

"I did not," Brynn told them. "I didn't have a dozen to waste."

"Well, you wasted a bunch," Jerusha said. "Didn't she, Boone?"

"Seems so."

"Obviously, you've improved since then," Jackson told her, handing the serving spoon to Jordan and smiling at her. He was sitting across the table from her and the window behind her reflected her back with the long braid to her hips very nicely.

"Thank you," she said and returned the smile.

"You lot look as if you are doing all right here by yourselves," he said, buttering his bread. "How's work, Boone?"

Brynn switched her mind off. When men starting talking work, she quit listening. She could never fathom why they wanted to work all day and then come home and talk about it all evening. She had no desire to do so, herself. So, while Boone told about life over at Carson's and Jordan talked about New House cattle and how many calves the Old House herd should have this spring, she mulled over how many clothes she would have to get ironed this evening before church the next day and whether she could politely tell Jackson when she needed him to leave so she could do so.

By the time Jackson was halfway into telling about Stephen Darcy and how the newspaper office was shaping up, she had decided that she didn't care if he was here, she had things to do. She and the other girls cleared the table, Jerusha was, with difficulty, persuaded to start the dishwater and Sorrel to dry, and she got out the iron, set it on the stove and took the end of the table for the ironing pad. Jackson asked her if she needed them to move, she replied not at all; if they didn't mind, she didn't, and the men went on with their conversation.

"That old guy, Denny, is as sharp a trader as I've ever seen," Jackson was going on. "Good thing too, since Steve would lose his shirt to the first vendor he came across. Not that Denny's not honest about it, but he got him a helluva deal on the printing press, even if it is second hand. You need to come out and see the place; he'll be ready to start printing the first edition in a week. Then he won't let anybody in; he'll be too busy."

"When are you going north to trap?" Jordan asked him.

"Got one more trip planned up into North Carolina, maybe to Kentucky in a couple weeks. Then that'll be it for the year," he replied.

"Wish I could go," Jordan sighed.

"Well, you can't," Brynn said and by their surprised looks, she knew that they had forgotten she was there. She flipped a shirt over on the pad and ran a crease up another sleeve. "You can't," she repeated. "You got work to do for New House. Planting's coming. You can't go anywhere."

"I **know** Brynn," the boy said. "I just said I wish."

"No sense wishing for something you can't have," she said. "You get wishing too hard about it, next thing I know, you'll be wandering off somewhere."

"All right," he said. "I get the idea."

After a bit, Boone asked if Jackson wanted to play some blackjack and the three of them went on playing well after Brynn finished the ironing for Sunday, the girls finished the dishes and tidied the kitchen, and all three had taken their leave; the girls upstairs and Brynn to the front room to darn Sorrel's gloves.

She wasn't very good at darning. Her Mama had been teaching her when she had died, and she had said that she would get better at it the longer she practiced. Brynn didn't like practicing something she wasn't good at, that was the trouble.

It was past eight-thirty, the back of her neck was beginning to ache and she had just about decided that she was going to call it a night, whether Jackson Flynn was gone or not, when Jackson himself came into the room. He stood a minute, then seemed to see her sitting in her Daddy's big wing chair back from the fire.

"There you are," he said.

"Yes, here I am," she replied, biting off a thread.

"Game over?"

Jackson was really a nice looking sort, he would still catch her attention even if he dressed like all the other farmers around Dooley, instead of the way he did. He moved with an easy confidence rather than the gangly way boys her age still had as if they didn't quite know where their arms and legs were. He was a man, not a boy, a man who had lived his own life for a long time, and it showed.

He came a few steps closer and stood before the fire. "Yes, I think I took all the money from those two that I care to," he replied.

"I hope you're joking," she said.

"I am," he replied, smiling. "Do you have enough light to see what you're doing? You'll go blind or something. Why don't you light the lamp?"

"Lamp oil costs money," she told him briskly. "Anyway, I'm finished now." She bundled Sorrel's gloves together and set them aside. "And I think I'm off to bed. It's getting late."

"Yes, I'm on my way, too," Jackson said. "I just wanted to say thanks. And ask if you wanted to go for a walk or something."

She regarded him. She didn't know it, but Jackson was thinking what a nice looking sort she was, too. He always had a time not staring at her too much. "Now?" she asked in surprise.

"Yes."

"It's a little late, isn't it?"

"It's Saturday. And we wouldn't be gone long."

"It's cold out there."

"We wouldn't be gone long," he repeated. "Where's your coat?"

Her Daddy would've never let her go doing this, she was thinking as five minutes later, they were strolling from the front porch toward the old dirt track that wound around Old House toward Long Barn. She doubted if her Mama would've even let her. But, she was her own person now, with nobody but herself to answer to---despite what Boone thought---and she took a certain perverse pleasure in doing something of which she knew her parents would not have approved.

It was cold out, as she knew it would be, but with her big coat on, her hands deep in the pockets and her scarf about her neck, she hardly felt it. Her heart was thumping too hard, the blood pumping through her kept her warm. She could practically feel the warmth of the man who walked beside her, his hands in his pockets, too. There was a little, crescent moon up above the trees.

"You know," Jackson said after a bit. "I think the bunch of you might just pull this off."

She looked up at him curiously. "What do you mean?"

"I mean this Old House venture you have here," he said. The cold puffed out white with his words. "You seem to be making it work for you. Seems as if everybody cooperates. It might just work."

"Well," she said. "We haven't been at it very long. And everybody **doesn't** cooperate all the time, believe me. Come by one Monday morning and you'll see what I mean. But, all we can do is try, I guess."

"You could just go live with your uncle," he pointed out.

She shook her head. "No, not if we can help it. Uncle Kevin's got some of Daddy's herd for us, did Jordan tell you?"

"Yes, he did. That's money on the hoof for you, right? By the way, speaking of Jimbo," he added. "I was thinking; how would it be if one weekend, I take him off your hands and take him with me when I go for a jaunt up in the hills. Just a couple nights, get him home in time for Monday morning."

Brynn didn't answer for a minute. Her dark eyes were obscured in the tricky light, but he could see that she had them narrowed at him. "Why?" she asked after a moment.

"He seems to need a lift, is all," he said. "He's good company. Give you a break from one of the younger ones."

"I don't need a break from Jordan," she replied. "I need him here to help."

"He looked like he might need a lift," he repeated.

"If anybody needs a lift, I do," she said dryly.

"All right," he said agreeably. "You want to come away with me for a weekend jaunt up into the hills?"

She looked away, but not before he saw her smile. "All right," she said. "It might do him good, I suppose. Wouldn't hurt anything. You get him back early Sunday night, though. He's got to be ready to get up Monday morning."

"I'll have him back early," Jackson promised.

They stopped where the dirt track started downhill toward the boundary with New House. The house was almost obscured by the trees here; there was an old, tumbled down fence that had been tumbled down even when they had first come to Old House. Brynn remembered her Daddy driving the covered wagon up that track---or trying to, at least. It had been deeply rutted, with big protruding rocks and deep pot holes.

Morgan had slapped the reins on the horses' backs and yelled at them and the lurch the wagon had taken had made Amy clutch the side of the seat and the twins bounce around in the back like popcorn. Jordan, with his hair curling up over his hat rim, had bounced and rolled around on the pallet in the wagon box twice as much as he needed to until Amy told him to stop. Brynn looked down the dark hill and sighed, her breath white in the still air.

"You're tired," Jackson said and there was a tone in his voice that made her look at him. "We'd best go back."

"I guess I am, a bit," she agreed as they turned toward the house again. "I guess that's why I'm as mean as a snake most of the time to the children."

"I don't see you as being mean to them," he told her. "I don't think they do, either."

She gave a short laugh. "You haven't seen us at our worst," she said. "It's a sight, I'll tell you. Mama would have us strapped for what goes on, I suppose. But it all just comes out, somehow."

"I think your Mama and Daddy would be proud of all of you," he said. "Especially you."

She looked at him with a tilted eyebrow. "Especially me? Why especially me?"

"You decided on all this, yes? The bunch of you living up here at Old House, making it on your own?"

"Yes," she admitted. "Such as it is."

"Well, then."

"But proud of me?" she shrugged. "I get more like Daddy every day. So Boone says."

"And that's bad, is it?"

She thought of her Daddy as he had been after his accident. How dark he had been, the flashes of temper, that one day when he had shoved Sorrel... "Sometimes it is. Most of the time, according to my Aunt Janny," she replied.

"I remember," Jackson said. Again she looked up at him, wondering. "Anyway," he added. "We all have our moments. Even me." He grinned.

"Even you, eh?"

"Yes, I'm not always the charming, happy-go-lucky fellow you see here," he said.

So then she smiled. The puppy-soft eyes crinkled at the edges, the downturn to her mouth disappeared, erasing the bitter look to it. She had a full, curved mouth, a decided cleft in the narrow chin and an unexpectedly small dimple that would appear suddenly, as it did now. "I never would have put the words Jackson Flynn and happy-go-lucky in the same sentence," she told him.

"I beg your pardon; and why not?"

"Well," she said. "Maybe 'secretive'. 'Unusual.'"

" 'Outrageously handsome'?"

"Maybe," she was really smiling now. She turned to face him, walking backward like a small child as they talked.

"Well, thank you, ma'am."

"And what would you use to describe me, then?" she asked him. "And be nice, now."

"To describe Brynn McKenna---let's see," he looked above her head toward the silhouette of the house before them. " 'Strong-minded.'"

"Yes."

" 'Courageous.'"

"Very good."

He looked down at her again. " 'Beautiful.'"

"Now, now, Mr. Flynn," she laughed at him. "Just because I fed you supper."

"No," he said. "Not because of that." He stopped walking and she stopped after a couple of more backward steps. She stood with her hands in her coat pockets and looked at him.

After a minute or two, he said: "Well, I have to go."

"Do you?"

In the muted light, she couldn't see his face well. The rim of his hat, the chin strap dangling, threw most of his face into shadow. He was just standing, looking at her. After a moment, he took a breath, stepped two steps to her and cupping her face in his hands, he kissed her mouth slowly. Brynn felt her own breath kick suddenly into her middle, a flash of a chill hitting just after.

He kissed her once, then once more, then put his arms about her and drew her up against him until her arms were around his neck and he was kissing her mouth in a strange, exploring way. She felt the chill inside her turn into heat and shiver out from her chest into the rest of her and she couldn't have stopped herself if her parents had both been out on the porch together.

After awhile, he stopped and stepped back from her. She kept hold of his arms; she was shaking. "I'm sorry," he said. "I shouldn't have started that."

"Wh-why?" she asked.

"Because...," he took another step back and she had to let him go. She hugged her arms about herself. "You don't need that right now," he said. "Maybe I don't, either."

She looked away then. Jackson felt his heart thudding in his chest, as he had felt hers against him a moment before. He watched her, watched the downcast eyes and they stood silent. It was quite dark, really. The one lighted window upstairs was a weak glow and never touched them.

"I'm not eight years old anymore, you know," she told him at length. Her gaze came up again, and met his from under those lashes.

"Yes, I know," he said. "But what I want to do with you is more than you can handle, even now."

She tilted her head at him. "And how would you know that, Jackson?" she asked. "You know practically nothing about me. How would you know?"

He really couldn't help it, so he went to her again and took her shoulders in his hands. She looked straight up into his eyes and, even in the near-dark, he was struck at how ferocious they were. He had always been struck by that. She was demure and quiet and ferocious underneath.

"Brynn," he said quietly to her. "You're seventeen. And I've wanted to do that for a long time. And that's all it is. I should've left. I should leave now. And I will."

"But you'll be back," she finished for him.

He kissed her again, she met him more than halfway, and he told himself that this was absolutely the last time he would go walking with her after dark. He was vaguely grateful that it was cold and they had their coats on rather than some balmy summer night with only a thin dress concealing her. He had a hard enough time stopping.

"You'll be back," she added when they could speak. "But will I be sitting here waiting on you? That's the question, isn't it?"

"I suppose it is," he conceded.

When he had left, Brynn went inside, closed the front door and stood in the dark room where the fire in the grate was burning very low. She stood a moment, then took off her coat and dropping it over the settee, stood still again. She looked at the fire, her arms tight around herself.

"Oh my goodness," she said softly.

Jackson went quickly and got his horse from where he had tied it outside Long Barn. He was as near to trembling as he ever was. He had had no idea when he came to Old House that evening, or even when he had walked outside into the dark with the girl, that he would have done what he had thought about doing all those years. It had shaken him. He had acted on it like some kid, and he was as shook up as if it was his first kiss.

Resolutely, he kicked his horse into a canter heading off of Old House land. Sooner away the better, he decided. He needed to go. He should've gone weeks before; instead he had dallied here in this hill-town as if he really had anything to stay for. Now he had crossed that line he had drawn for himself. He had thought he could keep it between him and her. He had done it all these years as she had grown up, even during the past months when her parents had died and she was on her own. Her father had been a strong deterrent, when he was gone, Jackson had had no strong pull toward her; no more than he had before, at least. What the hell had he been thinking?

He needed to go. He needed to go home. He needed to go back and make his peace with them. He still had things to sort out about Danny, to decide what to do about her, to finish grieving for Jonny. He needed to get things sorted out in his head before he went any further with anybody else.

-5-

Suddenly, the weather changed.

As it often did in the hills, winter hadn't really started until the new year, and the bad weather didn't start until February. Now, as well as the cold, there was sleet and flurries of snow that came and went, and cold, not-quite-freezing rain during the day that changed to a slippery coating over everything at night. Brynn went to work anyway. She didn't like it, but she did. She needed the money and only a blizzard would have kept her home.

The children struggled to school in the cold. Sorrel developed a cough that rasped far down in her chest and which she never seemed to get rid of. Every morning, Brynn felt her head and looked into her throat although she had no idea what she was looking at, and every day she sent her on off to school. When the weekend came, she let Sorrel sleep in and skip church and skimp on her chores and altogether spoiled her, as Jerusha indignantly informed her.

"She needs a doctor," Boone said in a quiet moment.

"I think she's better," Brynn replied, although she could feel the worry lines in her forehead. She mixed up cider vinegar and honey, set the kettle of hot water in her room at night and wrapped her throat in flannel, but as yet, the doctor was just out of her reach.

"At least let Janny come take a look at her," Boone said.

"No," she replied. Then, at her brother's expression, hearing the girl start coughing again, she added: "If she's no better by the middle of the week, I will."

"If you'd let the fire be lit in her room, it'd help," he observed. He was getting ready for work.

"Woodpile's running low," she replied. "Unless you want to take a day off and cut some more falls, drag them up here and split it, we have to make do. Winter ain't half over yet."

"Shit," Boone said, and left.

He went across the river to Carson's in a mood. He wished he could just over-ride Brynn and go to Janine, then ride into town to see Dr. Banks and send them both to see to Sorrel. Then, he would probably stop by Wilkes' and get a load of firewood sent over all split and stacked to finish things off.

He wished he could, but he knew he wouldn't. Boone had a great respect for protocol, and all at Old House had agreed—in principal, if not in so many words—that Brynn was head of the house. What she said went, at least until he thought her decisions were sending them over a cliff. They weren't quite to the cliff stage yet. Getting close, but not over the edge.

Work on Carson's farm in the cold wasn't pleasant these days. There weren't many hands during the winter months, not near as many as at harvest or roundup in the fall when the herd was sent to auction and the migrant workers were hired.

Boone knew he couldn't complain. To be kept on all year was a good thing, and showed that Sam Carson liked his work, but it also meant that he was jack of all trades and was ordered to do almost anything that the two Carson boys, Cale and Seth didn't want to do. Especially Cale. Cale, as the eldest son, was next in command to Sam and wasn't afraid of letting anyone know it. Boone tried to keep out of his way.

Winter meant repairs around the farm, and the farm included the Big House itself. Still worried about Sorrel, Boone took little interest in the discussion going on outside the main barn as he went about the regular barn chores that only the most menial help did when there were many workers, but that was assigned to him now. He pitched soaked hay and manure from the stalls to the wheelbarrow with only part of his attention on what he was doing, hearing the voices of the boss and his sons going on outside. If he had been so inclined, he could have seen them through the half-open door, smoke wafting from Sam's thick cigar, but he didn't bother.

"All right then," Sam at last said, turning and stepping over the sill into the barn itself, pushing the door open as he did. "Seth, take McKenna with you. Will, you and Cale and Toby and Comfort go get to work on that far shed. We'll get what we can do while the weather holds off."

Boone glanced up at the sound of his name as he finished the stall. Sam Carson was dressed like a working farmer, not a gentleman one, but the coat that fell nearly to his boot tops was thickly expensive and his boots, although a muddy as Boone's own, were the best.

"McKenna," he said, around the cigar. "When you're finished in here, go with Seth up to the house and see if the two of you can pin down where that leak is in the attic. With the weather we had yesterday, you should be able to tell. Should be damp up there. My wife is giving me up the country about finding it and getting it fixed before that dinner party she's got planned. You about done?"

"Two more," Boone replied.

"All right, then. Get a move on and be sure to give the big box stall good thick bedding. She's my best brood mare and this foal'll come early or I miss my guess."

"Yes, sir," Boone said.

When he had finished and was walking with Sam's youngest son, Seth, up the hill toward the Big House, Seth said, jerking a thumb back where Cale was walking the other way: "He ain't happy you pulled house duty, but I imagine my sister will be."

Boone looked at him questioningly, then back at the group of men headed toward one of the outbuildings. Cale was a square, imposing figure, several years Boone's senior, as blunt-headed, square-set, blond, and blue-eyed as any Norseman. Seth, the younger of the two, but still older than Boone, was taller and slender but with the broad-shoulders that outdoor work in all weather built, his hair tended to more of the streaked brown and his temperament was more civilized than his moody brother.

Seth grinned at his look. "Oh, come on now, McKenna," he said. "Surely you must know that Schuyler's feelings for you are common knowledge. Of course, Schuyler had 'feelings' for a good many men, but you seem to have her in a quandary most of the time. Which is a good thing. Good to keep the girl guessing. Her Daddy approves of that. And of you. And that means, of course, that brother Cale don't approve of you at all. But Cale has trouble approving of anyone, most of the time. Don't let it worry you."

"I won't," Boone assured him.

The fact was that Schuyler Carson was a subject that he only allowed his mind to dwell on late at night or the few other times that he had nothing else pressing on his consciousness. That meant that he didn't think of her any more than absolutely necessary.

Before the new year and the family moving into Old House, he had had occasion to observe the girl from time to time at a distance, and a few times up close, but he hadn't pursued the opportunity. He had more than enough to occupy his mind and time these days with the group across the river. He had decided that he wasn't going to cloud things with some girl.

His parents had died in September, he seemed to not recall much of anything until about November and Schuyler had kept out of his way after the one encounter he had had with her in the bunk house with Rhodes. She was giving him his space, but Boone neither realized it or much cared.

At Thanksgiving, the first since he lost his parents, he had ridden home from dinner at New House and had passed an enclosed buggy on the road. Schuyler Carson had been inside with a well-dressed young man and, as he reined in Roanoke off the road to let them pass, he had caught a glimpse of them, recognized them, and touched his hat brim to her. He didn't sit and watch them go, however, although he had seen the girl's smile fade at the sight of him. He didn't see her look back at him through the small window, or know how he had affected the rest of her evening.

He had been tired and drained by trying to make Thanksgiving day festive for the little ones and ready to get in his bunk. That the son of one of Esther Carson's friends was escorting Schuyler to dinner with her mother's full, hopeful approval didn't matter to him at all. He didn't know that the sight of him, sitting his horse in the misty cold, the glimpse of his face showing Schuyler how tired he was, would color the lush atmosphere of the home where she spent the next few hours, or the bright, shallow people that lived there.

By Christmas, he had almost been able to dislodge her from his mind completely. It was a silly thing, really, entertaining any idea of the girl. She was the boss's daughter---a very wealthy, old-family, only daughter at that---he was a hired hand, the son of an Irish farmer and half-Cajun mother. Things like that didn't happen, not really. No matter what the girl had said to him in the summer before, by this time she would have been persuaded otherwise, either by her parents or by some more suitable man.

So, he didn't think much of it when, a few days before Christmas, in passing below the back stoop and seeing Ginny, the cook's helper struggling with an armload of wood, he stopped and took it from her to carry it up the steps and into the kitchen. He had no reason to think that she would be anywhere around, so it was a bit of a shock when he put the wood into the box and was laughingly replying to something Ginny was saying, to turn and see Schuyler standing there.

He fumbled in what he was saying, brushed himself off, and said something more or less appropriate before taking his leave. The sight of her so close had done something to him.

He had been almost off the back porch and was starting down the steps when she called to him. He stopped and she hesitated. He didn't know then, any more than he had at Thanksgiving, that his sudden appearance had shaken her, too.

At length, she came down the long back porch, nearly dark as it was and he saw that she was dressed for dinner. They all dressed for dinner at the Big House, he knew. He had seen them, had seen Sam himself who hated above all things to have to stop work to dress up, dressed in his tie and jacket at dinner time. Schuyler's skirt rustled as she came across the porch to him and he saw light sparkle at her throat and ears. A wafting sweet scent came from her.

"I just wanted to say Merry Christmas," she said and she was a bit breathless.

"Oh," he replied. "Well. Merry Christmas to you, too."

"Even though it's not for four more days," she added and laughed a little.

"That's true," he allowed.

He stepped back up onto the porch from his move down the stairs. Now he was close to her, he was looking down into her face and she didn't step back from him. The dress was cut in a scoop away from her shoulders and showed a glow of fair skin below her throat. After a moment, she asked:

"How are you? How is your family? All your brothers and sisters?"

And he could tell that she really wanted to know.

"They're...," he hesitated, then decided to say the truth. "I don't know how they are," he admitted. "It's been months, I know. But it's Christmas and it's hard on them, I suppose."

"And hard on you," she added for him.

"Yes, I guess so," he said.

"What I told you before," she said. "You know, about if you ever need to talk to anyone, it still stands. If you want to talk about anything, you can look me up. Or," she said. "even if you don't want to talk, but just to ---be---you can. I---I don't mean---you know---like you found me that—that—time with---I don't mean that..."

"I know," he told her and smiled at her to show that he really did. "Thanks. I appreciate that."

And they had said good-night and he had left. He had tried, since then, to go back to thinking of her as just the boss's daughter, to believing that there was another suitor in her life that would, some day soon, be announcing that she had consented to marry him, with all parents' approval, but somehow, now he knew that it wasn't true.

He had seen the look in her eye that night. And, although he left her strictly alone, and had left the thought of her for only the most fleeting of imaginings, still Seth's words this day gave him pause. And the thought of walking into the Big House and possibly seeing her, colored the dreary day in a whole new way.

The Big House had another, more elaborate name; one that was recognized in the county. Big, Southern homes were always named as a custom of the area and the class of owner, but the hired help had always just called it the Big House, and as time went on, the family found itself doing the same. And Boone had never failed to be impressed by the sheer established opulence of the place.

He knew that the parties given there were famous in the area, he had been witness to the preparations to a few, and when he had lived at the bunk house, he had seen carriage after carriage sweeping in at the lane to a house ablaze with lights. He had been assigned to handle the driving teams when they were brought around to the barns to wait. The drivers of the carriages—tall, well-dressed black men---were far above him in rank, and looked down on the farm help with suspicion when he came forward to take the heads of the horses.

"You be careful wid dat hoss, boy," he would be told. "Dat hoss worth more'n you by five-hundred dollars." Then, to each other, he would hear: "Dem Irish boys, dey taking over the country. An' dat one look half Injun, too. I keep my eye on dat one wid my boss's hoss."

Boone didn't really care. He knew that he moved in a different culture that the Carsons. The hill people were a class unto themselves, and he, although not born to it, had been accepted into it and now was one with them. He knew that to the Carsons, at least to Esther and Cale, he would always be a "local", the term later known as hillbilly. As far as Boone was concerned, if that made him invisible to them, so much the better.

But the encounter at Christmastime, and now Seth's words made him know that Schuyler thought of him in a different light. He followed Seth into the kitchen of the Big House, where it was warm and smelled of dinner cooking and where Cook and Ginny were flitting around. Seth spoke to them, they stopped and curtseyed to the boss's son as they passed through, and then they made their way out into the back hall where the narrow stairs came down in shadows from the servants' wing.

"We'll get the tools and go up the back way," Seth told him over his shoulder, leading the way into one of the many little rooms off the back hall.

These were the "big pantries" where rows of shelves held crocks of preserves and cider, vinegar and sauerkraut, and, behind wire screens sat shelves of serving trays, tall urns for hot coffee, ornate carved serving vessels of all types. The massive fireplaces had thick-walled insets for bread-baking, there were tall churns and cupboards full of all the china only used at the best dinners. Seth led the way to the back of one of these rooms where the biggest enclosed cupboard held the household tools.

Boone had never seen such organization. Everything was labeled, every shelf had its own use and everything was put in its proper place. With difficulty, he kept his wits about him enough to take up the tool box that Seth indicated, filled it with what they would likely need, and followed him out toward the back steps.

And on the landing as they prepared to turn toward the attic stairs, they met Schuyler herself. It was only after a moment that Boone realized that Esther Carson was also with her, followed closely by two young maids with arms full of folded linen. His eyes went straight to the girl and hers to him and he returned her smile.

"Gracious, Seth!" Esther said and drew her skirts aside. "Look at you! I do hope you wiped your feet carefully before you came into the house. Where are you going, anyway? And don't get near the linens. They're just in from Charleston."

"We're going to try to find the leak that you wanted Pa to find," Seth told her. "Morning, ladies," he added to the maids and tipped his hat. He had the type of smile that girls found so appealing. The maids giggled. "And yes, Mother, our feet are as clean as they can be under the circumstances."

Esther gave the maids a glance that brought instant decorum and, as she did, she saw Schuyler's face. "Well," she said. "Just be sure you find it, please. The party is in three weeks, and the last thing I need is a lot of workmen tramping in and out spreading mud and sawdust and knocking plaster off the ceilings with all that hammering as we're trying to prepare." She looked at Boone as if sure he would be the one doing such things, then swept by them on her way to the west wing. "Come along, Schuyler," she added.

As he and Boone went on their way up the tight curve of the attic stairs, Seth said over his shoulder: "New maid, I see. Not bad. There's possibilities. My mother seems right fond of you, I must say."

"Yes, I noticed that, too," Boone replied.

It took most of the morning to find the leak and to ascertain how bad the damage was from the wet. Boone was amazed at the attic of the Big House. It was as immense as an attic for a house that size would be expected to be, but the lines of trunks, the old furniture, and stored bric-a-brac was beyond him.

There was a high peak that followed the line of the roof above the front doors and upstairs balcony and here was an ornately shaped window for light, as well as two skylights in the roof itself. It was around one of these windows that the water was leaking and had damaged a good part of the frame as well as the flooring below.

"Which probably means that the ceiling below that is shot, too," Seth remarked, ripping at rotten wood with the claw of his hammer. "Mother will be thrilled with the mess we'll have to make to get all that fixed. And Pa won't be too happy, either." He looked down at Boone from the step. "You want the job of telling them?"

"Your father, I wouldn't mind," he replied. "Your mother is another story."

Seth grinned and said he didn't blame him.

As they worked together on tearing out wet wood, Boone noticed something interesting. He waited until they were about halfway through, then mentioned it to Seth.

"You noticed that, too, did you?" Seth said. "Well, don't say that you have to anybody. The rest of the family wouldn't take too kindly that you knowing about it. I asked Pa about it once and he about took my head off. There's a good four foot bump-out on this side of the wall, and another couple feet in the stairwell. Don't know why."

It was true, Boone saw now. He had seen the discrepancy under the ladder to the skylight; part of the wall protruded out into the attic, ran about eight feet toward the sloping rafters, then turned back and met the wall again at a ninety degree angle.

On the other side of the door that led downstairs, he could see another wall that came out into the stairwell by a good two feet, ran the same length as the inside wall, and stopped as the stair turned the corner downward. There was no door, no handle or anything to indicate that there ever had been one. There was just a boxed-off section in the attic. He shrugged and went on with the work.

They had about decided they had done all the damage they could do without Sam's approval when there was a step on the stairs and Schuyler came into the dusky room, a tray in her hands. Boone came forward and took it from her.

"Thanks," she said, smiling at him. "Thought you two might want something to drink; you've been slaving away up here so long."

There were two dewy glasses of buttermilk. Seth took one and as Boone handed the tray back to her, he said: "Thank you," and took a moment to appreciate how close they were to each other. "Where's yours?" he added.

"Oh, I've had mine," she told him. "When Cook does the churning, I'm first in line for buttermilk, don't worry."

He drank, standing back from her, watching as she and Seth talked about the leak and the rotten wood, bantering back and forth as he did with his own siblings. At last, Seth said:

"Well, I'd better go down and get the old man and see what he says." He gave them a look and added: "You two behave yourselves. I'll be right back." And winked at Boone.

When he had gone, Schuyler said: "That was unusually nice of him."

"Was it?" he asked.

"Yes," she replied.

"Why?"

"Because he knows that I wanted to be with you a minute," she said. "Alone."

Now that she had him, she wasn't sure what to do with him. She knew she looked well in her everyday dress that suited her best. She knew he would like her better in an everyday dress, rather than one of the many more expensive dresses hanging in her wardrobe. She knew he would even like the fact that she still had her apron on, with the high bib and sash tied in the back. Her hair was bundled up out of her way and a few tendrils were coming loose about her face, and she knew he didn't mind that at all, either.

Boone, himself, was the way she liked him best; in his work clothes and slightly sweaty and smelling of leather and horses. Her mother would never understand, any more than Schuyler herself did, except that a man in that state reminded her of her father and that appealed to her much more than the elegant young men in their elegant clothes with smooth, gentlemen's hands like the ones who had been escorting her to her mother's friends' houses.

None of them had Boone's soft dark hair and eyes with the brows that swooped above them, the broodiness around the mouth that could change so astonishingly when he smiled. And none of them made her feel so breathlessly confused.

He was smiling now, at her last words. "Alone with me?" he said. "We're hardly alone, with your father on his way up and your mother one floor away, ready to pounce and drag you off if she knew."

She smiled too then. "My mother is downstairs telling Cook how she didn't like the compote last night," she replied. "So she's two floors away."

"Too far away to hear you scream for help then, when I knock you down and take advantage of you."

"Is that what you plan on doing, sir?"

"I'm trying to restrain myself," he told her.

"I am, too," she said. "Trying to restrain myself, that is."

"Are you? Are you about to knock me down, too?"

"Possibly," she told him.

Strange how at ease they both felt with each other in light of the last time they had had any kind of real conversation. Besides the encounter they had had on the back porch at Christmas, the last time had been in the bunkhouse when he had caught her with Rhodes. That had been a real conversation, she supposed.

She had been half-dressed, distraught, and totally humiliated, she had blurted out that she loved him. He had taken her hands in his, after speaking angrily to her, and had told her as gently as a father or as a brother, that she had to---had to---stop what she persisted in doing, and then finished her off by saying to not approach him again until she had grown up. A lot. And yet, despite all that, here they were.

"I'm afraid my mother doesn't approve of you," she said at length.

"No, I gathered that," he replied.

"My brother Cale doesn't think much of you, either. But Seth says you're all right. And Pa likes you fine."

"I'm proud to hear that," Boone said. "Since I'm on your father's payroll." He was silent, then added: "And what do you think of me, then?"

She looked at him in surprise. She never knew what to expect from him.

"Last fall, you were pretty blunt about it," he said. "I was just wondering."

"I said I loved you," she said.

"That you did."

"And you said that you had no time for me. That things were---too complicated for you right then."

"Something like that, if I recall," he agreed.

"So, are things still complicated?"

"At home? Things are always complicated. With you and me? Maybe not as much. Are they?"

She couldn't take her eyes away from him. "I don't---I don't know. I hope they're not. You're the one who said for me to look you up after I grew up some. I don't know if I have or not."

What he might have said to that she didn't know, for at that moment there were voices below and Sam Carson came climbing the attic steps, followed by Seth. When they reached the dim-lit room, Boone was across the floor from Schuyler, under the skylight as if he hadn't been within twenty feet of her.

Sam looked the place over, listened to Seth's explanation, nodded and said: "Well, hellfire. Looks like a full day's work we got in front of us. Probably two or three." He looked at Boone. "You up to working a hammer for a bit, instead of out in the pasture?"

"Yes, sir. Wherever you need me," he replied.

"Well, you and Seth seem to be started pretty good. I'll send Comfort up after awhile and give you a hand and the three of you finish the job. Get down below and see how much of that ceiling needs tearing out. Your mother'll probably pitch a fit, but can't be helped. And get up on the roof and see what you can see from that side. But tie yourself off to that chimney, whichever one of you goes out there. You hear me, Seth?"

"Yes, sir."

"No sense in anybody breaking their neck," he turned to leave, chucked Schuyler under the chin at the door and was almost out when Boone made up his mind.

"Boss?" he said, coming to stand beside her. The big man turned back then and Boone didn't look at the girl. He could feel her quite close to him. "Mr. Carson," he said. "I wanted to ask you something."

Sam looked at him, then at Seth and back at the girl. "Well?" he asked. "What is it, then?"

"I wanted to ask if I could call on your daughter, sir," Boone said.

He heard a little intake of breath from Schuyler. Sam's gaze flicked to her at the sound; Boone was sure he could see how the question had surprised her. Out of the corner of his eye, he could see Seth start to grin. Sam shifted on his ponderous feet, his boot-length camel's hair coat catching the spasmodic light in fawns and browns.

"Call on my daughter?" he asked.

"Yes, sir."

"Well," he said. In an instant, Boone knew what the answer would be. He knew it would be no. "I think that would be quite fine," he replied. "So, yes, you may." He turned and took two steps down the stairs then added over his shoulder. "Plan on coming to supper sometime pretty soon, too."

"Yes, sir," Boone said. "Thank you, sir."

"And if you run across Mrs. Carson," he said. "You best keep your guard up."

"Yes, sir," Boone replied. "I will."

He waited till Sam had turned the corner of the stairs before he looked at Schuyler. "I think maybe you have," he said. "Grown up, that is. A bit."

Sam was all the way to the back hall before Schuyler caught up to him. "Papa?" He turned and smiled at the sight of her, as he always did. She looked flushed and pretty, her eyes all sparkling. She tiptoed and kissed his cheek. "Thank you, Papa," she said softly.

He patted her face gently with one huge, rough hand. "You're welcome, baby," he replied.

"You like him, don't you, Papa?" she asked.

"I like him all right," he told her. "I knew his father. I know his uncle, over there across the river. Honest men. Nice family. And he works well. Never had any trouble with him. He'll do." He leaned down to add: "Better than that namby-pamby Rodgers boy, right?"

She nodded. "Yes, sir. Lots better. Papa?"

"What, honey?"

"You'll talk to mother, won't you? If she kicks up a fuss?"

He cocked an eyebrow at her in mock severity and Schuyler widened her eyes at him.

"Go on with you," he said. "We'll see who talks to who. And leave those boys up there alone, now. They got work to do."

"Yes, sir, Pa," Schuyler replied.

By the end of the week, the snow suddenly came.

Brynn struggled to work, anyway, rather relishing it, in fact. Angelina's hooves threw snow in fairy clouds as she trotted, snorting white. They took the high road up over the hill and looked down a town covered in a foot and a half of white. The next night, a blast of frigid air blew in sleet to coat the world in ice and then another unexpected six inches of snow fell.

School was closed and Sorrel's cough got better, Brynn was relieved to find when she came skidding home that evening. In fact, she found the three younger ones outside snowballing each other ferociously as she stabled Angelina and tramped up the hill from Long Barn.

"I hope you got supper ready before you came out here," she called to them. "And don't you dare, Jimbo!" she added as he made to heave a handful of snow at her.

"Aw, spoil sport," he said, chucking it at his twin, instead. "Guess what, Bernie."

"What?"

"Kate brought up a cake and some biscuits."

"That was white of her," Brynn replied as she went in the door.

There was leftover stew on the stove and Brynn had to admit, the biscuits were a heavenly addition, with layer cake for dessert. It was quite a nice evening, actually. Boone was in an angelic frame of mind, the children were thrilled with being off of school, except Jerusha who would prefer school over anything, and Sorrel was better.

They lingered over supper, all of them, and Jordan made them laugh with his impersonations of the neighbors in town until Jerusha fell out of her chair. At the end of it, when Brynn was pumping water into the sink for the dishes, Boone fished in his pocket and handed her an envelope.

"Forgot I had this," he said. "Geneva Willis gave it to me today when I saw her in town. Had to get some shingles for Carson at the hardware and saw her. She says you got to come."

"To what?" Brynn wiped her hands and took the little square envelope.

"Some party she's giving. She says that if the Carsons can give parties, she can too."

Brynn tore it open, read the little card and set it aside.

"Well?" Boone asked her.

"Well, what?"

"Well, what'd it say?"

"It's an invitation."

Boone looked put out. "I know that. When?"

"This weekend."

"You going?"

"No," she said.

"Why not?"

"Why not? What do you care? I don't want to. I haven't been asked. I don't want to, that's why."

He leaned on the counter and watched her slide dishes into the sink. "You would go if you got asked."

"Yes? How do you know that?"

"Because I know you. If Jack Flynn was to ask you…"

"Yes, well, Jackson Flynn is gone out of town, in case you haven't noticed," she turned to scrape out the dregs of the stew pot for Tommycat, but Boone had seen her face.

"He'll be back," he told her. "He always comes back."

She didn't answer. After a moment, he added:

"Why don't you go, anyway?"

She looked over her shoulder at him in amusement. "Why are you so interested in me going? You go if you're that interested in it."

"I'm not invited."

"It's for all of us, you know it is. At least, for the older ones of us. You and me."

"Well, I've got bigger fish to fry, thank you. And you ought to go. Geneva's a friend of yours, right? So you ought to go."

She didn't answer and after a minute, Boone left in disgust.

And then, it wasn't ten minutes later when Stephen Darcy knocked on the door. Jordan answered it, let him into the front room and yelled: "Brynn! Somebody here!" making Stephen put a finger in his ear. "She'll be here in a minute," Jordan added, more quietly. "Sit down if you want to." He hesitated, then asked: "You're that Darcy fellow, ain't you? That's starting that newspaper?"

Stephen removed his hat and replied: "Yep. That's me. Bout ready to print."

"Can I come look at the printing press sometime?"

"Sure," he said agreeably. "Any time before the end of the month. I'll be too busy then."

Brynn appeared at the door, wiping her hands on her apron. "Oh," she said. "Hello."

Stephen smiled at her. "Good evening."

She looked astonished to see him. She glanced down at herself; at her apron splashed with wet, then touched her hair that was wisping loose from the braid wound about her head. Jordan settled on the arm of the settee, chewed a toothpick and watched.

"Nice night," Stephen said conversationally.

"Is it?" she replied. "A little cold to be out riding around."

"Well," he said. "I wasn't quite out just riding around. I wanted to come ask you something."

"You did?"

"Yes," he said. "Could I---um---?"

"Oh, grief yes," she said. "Take off your coat and come on back in the kitchen. You want coffee?"

"Sure," he followed her into the big, open kitchen, dropping his coat and hat to a chair.

"I wouldn't be too excited about coffee," Jordan told him, trailing after them. "Brynn made it."

"Shush, Jimbo," his sister said as Stephen looked at him questioningly. "So you came all out here to ask something?" she said, getting down cups and turning to the coffee pot. "Must be something mighty important."

"Could be," Stephen admitted. "I wanted to know if you're going to the Willis party."

She sloshed in pouring and set the pot down hurriedly. "The Willis party?"

"Yes, surely you know about it. Everybody in town's invited, I hear."

"Not me," Jordan said.

"Jordan," Brynn said. "Do you mind? Stefan's talking to me."

"S'my house, too," he replied. "I got a right to be here."

"Anyway," Stephen said. "Since Jack Flynn's out of town, I was wondering if you have a date for the party yet."

Jordan grinned broadly around the toothpick from his position on the window seat behind Stephen's back. Brynn, with difficulty, didn't look at him. "A date?"

"And if you don't," he added. "I was wondering if you'd give me the pleasure. Of going with me, that is."

"Oh," she said in surprise. "Oh. Do you—do you take cream and sugar? In your coffee?"

"Sure," he replied cheerfully. "Whichever. Or both. So, would you? Go with me to the party?"

He seemed to have really thrown her by his question. It was endearing how she was bumbling around with the milk pitcher and all, and how her brother was enjoying it. Stephen was enjoying her confusion, too, if it came to that. When she at last slid the cup across to him and he was stirring it, she said:

"My goodness."

"You thought nobody would ask you?"

"I only just heard about it," she told him.

There was a sound suddenly on the stairs like a herd of buffalo crashing down them, and the two younger McKenna girls came dashing in. The littler one, with the long dark hair, pulled up abruptly and the other one ran into the back of her, but didn't stop what she was saying.

"Brynn, I'm not going to clean up her mess this time!" she was saying loudly. "and don't let her tell you nothing. I didn't do it!"

"She did, too, Sister," the littler one said. She was smiling at Stephen with eyes like Brynn's, and Stephen returned it. "She joggled my arm. I didn't mean to spill it."

The blonde one noticed him and paused long enough to say: "Oh, hey. And I did not, and you know it! She sloshed it all over and I ain't cleaning it up. There's milk from one end of the bed to the other, and it's in **my bed**, too! Tell her, Brynnie! Tell her she's got to clean it up."

"What was milk doing up in your room, anyway?" Brynn demanded. "You know the rule. No food upstairs, since you found that mouse. And you spilled milk? Rue! You know we don't have that much till we get the milk from Katie."

"I did not spill it!"

"Well, if it was your milk…"

"It wasn't mine!"

"…then you're the one who's going without, that's all."

"Brynnie!" Jerusha said shoving Sorrel in retaliation as she put her tongue out at her. "It was her milk and she spilled it!"

"I did not."

"And even if it was, you said no **food**. And it wasn't food."

"The two of you get out of here," Jordan told them. "Brynn's getting asked out on a date."

"Really?" Sorrel asked, turning those big brown eyes on him. "So are you going to go, Sister?"

"There's milk all over my bed," Jerusha went on. "It's all soaky wet. Who's going to clean it up?"

"It's your bed," Brynn told her. "You clean it up."

"Where're y'all going?" Sorrel asked Stephen.

"There's a party in town," he told her. Then, he asked: "How old are you?"

"Thirteen," she replied.

"Like blue hell you are," Jerusha told her. "You're twelve."

"Stop that," Brynn said. "Go clean up your room. Sorrel, you too. Go help. Both of you scat."

"I'm almost thirteen," Sorrel said to Stephen and sneezed.

"Bless you," he replied, smiling at her. "And you're still too young."

"I won't be forever," she said, over her shoulder as Jerusha dragged her by her elbow toward the stairs again.

"So," Stephen said at last when they had gone. He took a drink of his coffee, nearly didn't swallow it, then recovered. "What do you say?"

Brynn was twisting the dishcloth, biting her lip, then seemed to make up her mind. "All right," she said. "It might be fun."

"It will be fun," Stephen said to her.

And it was. Most of it, at least, she allowed. In years to come, she would look back on it and appreciate it all, but at the time, it was different.

Geneva Willis' family was one of the most established, well-off in Dooley. Rather than the Carsons' wealth and old family connections, the Willis's were born and raised hill family who had been frugal, educated their children and yet had never left their roots.

Now, Ben Willis had a large, but not ornate, house with plenty of land, a thriving business in town and five daughters who wore their father's wealth with good grace and were friendly to all. The girls were all miniatures of their mother; plump, short and as rosy as any Dutch matron, even the youngest. Geneva was the middle child and she and Brynn had been friends for years.

Ben Willis could deny his daughters nothing, and the party had been hastily planned when the snows came and the small pond below their house had frozen. Every young person in town had been invited to skate and sled that Friday evening; a three piece band had even been hired, food provided and an enormous bonfire built on the shore.

The Willis girls and their mother together with several hired help were scurrying about. There was hot chocolate in a big iron kettle over the fire, cider in another, roast apples, chestnuts and popcorn to finish it off. There was steaming roast pig and roast beef sliced on the huge slab of table nearby, and altogether enough food to "feed the town" as Ben Willis proudly announced when he greeted the guests driving up his lane.

"Get on down at the pond," he said, waving one burly arm. " 'Nuff food down there for everybody. Glad to see you, glad to see you. You're all welcome."

There were quite a few cutters in Dooley, mostly homemade, because deep snows were not unheard of this far into the hills, despite it being in Georgia. There even a few sleighs of two rows of seats, but these were the wealthier families. Stephen came to pick Brynn up in his father's cutter, handed her in, tucked her in with lap-robes as if she was an infant, and asked if she was warm enough.

Brynn had to admit that this was more like it: getting dressed, if not exactly in her best, at least in her second best; getting treated with respect for a change; going out for an evening. She and Boone both had been fussing about getting ready, although Boone declared he wasn't going to the Willis'. Nevertheless, he had wheedled Brynn into ironing his shirt while she was struggling to tack up a rip in her hem, had hogged the mirror hanging in the kitchen just as she needed it, and had made a few lurid references to Stephen Darcy just to make her mad. She had been quite glad that he had left before she had.

It was all like a dream, Brynn decided as she drove with Stephen across the snow. It was so blue-white and glowing in the moonlight, the smell of the air so different, then the scene down by the frozen pond as they came over the rise, was like a painting of light and color against the chilly backdrop. Everyone seemed to be there, that was sure, including her cousin, Clay, with Geneva herself on his arm, and most of her old friends from school who she hadn't seen since the new year. Stephen pulled the sleigh to a stop among the others, got out and covered the horse with the blanket, and still she couldn't stop looking at it all.

"Brynn?" Stephen said, then, when she looked down at him, he asked: "You ready?"

"Yes," she replied, and, smiling at him, she took his hand as he helped her down.

And the first ones she saw was Clay, of course with Geneva. He came across to them, introduced everybody all around, joked with Stephen, teased Brynn and was altogether the same as he always was. Clay was always the one who made everybody feel at ease, he was the one people thought of first as being invited to anything.

Geneva took hold of Brynn's elbow and pulled her aside. Her rosy, cherubic face under its knit hat was excited. She had very yellow, very curly hair that pushed its way out from under her hat, framing her face until she looked like an illustration in a picture book.

"Brynnie, so that's Steve Darcy," she said. "Don't you look precious," she added, taking a look at her appraisingly. "I love that dark red on you. So that's Steve Darcy---didn't we know him in school a long time ago?"

"I think so," Brynn replied rather vaguely.

"And he's starting a newspaper," she went on. "I hear his grandmother's really rich. Is she? She's the one you work for, right? Is she really rich?"

"I don't know. I don't think so."

"Well, I think he's just too cute," Geneva said firmly. "And your cousin, Clay is too. I don't remember him being that cute---Clay, I mean. He's so much fun. Are you going to skate?"

"I suppose," Brynn told her. "You think Clay's cute?"

"Absolutely," Geneva's blue eyes were wide and sincere. Geneva was always sincere, that was one thing for sure. If she told you a thing was true, then, as far as Geneva was concerned, it was true. Brynn looked at Clay and Stephen laughing together. She couldn't see her cousin as being cute, but then he was just not at all like Adam, that was certain.

Stephen, now, she added to herself, forcing her gaze back; Stephen was not bad at all. He always seemed to be all put together, somehow, to carry himself as if he knew exactly what he was doing and where he was going. There was something attractive in that.

"Brynnlin," Clay said to her. "You and Steve come skate, me and Neeva will skate and that'll get everybody else doing it."

So they did. Brynn decided, right then, that no matter what, she was going to have a good time that night. She hung onto Stephen's arm until she got her sea legs, then they skated and swung each other around and played crack the whip with four or five others until she could hardly breathe for laughing. She fell down and got pulled back up and shoved Clay into the snow and then couldn't get away fast enough and got her face washed with a handful until Geneva rescued her.

By the time they stopped to rest, the pond was full of people. There were a few little ones and Stephen took a cup of hot chocolate to one little girl who had fallen down and was being comforted by her mother. Then, he brought Brynn one, too and she smiled up at him, thinking how nice that was of him.

She blew on her steaming cup and asked how the newspaper was coming along.

"Start printing end of the month," he told her with that smile that made him very handsome, really. "Monday morning next, the first edition comes out. You'll buy a copy?"

"Me? Not me. Not unless you're giving them away," she replied.

"Won't make much money if I do that," he said. "Maybe I'll bring one by my grandmother's for you to see."

She laughed. "Don't do that if you value your head. You know how your grandmother feels about that newspaper business."

"Then, I'll bring one by for Rosemary," he said. "And to heck with my grandmother."

"Then come to the back door," she warned him.

"Ah, but then I might not get to see you," he said.

"You'd risk the wrath of Mrs. Darcy for me? I'm flattered, Stefan."

"Why do you persist in calling me that?" he asked.

"What?"

"Stefan. Why do you keep calling me that?"

Those brown eyes of hers could slant like a cat's at times, he was thinking, watching her looking up at him over her cup as she drank. Then, at times like this, they were big and soft and sweet as a baby's.

"That's your name, isn't it?" she countered.

"My name's Stephen Christopher, if you want to get specific," he said. "Grandmother's the only one who always insists on calling me Stefan; until now, that is. That was my grandfather's name. I suppose that's why she does it."

"And I do it because she does it," Brynn said comfortably. "So, I suppose you'll just have to put up with it. Is that all right, Mr. Darcy?"

He said of course, it was. They drank their chocolate, then they went back out until Clay challenged them to a sledding race and then they sledded until Geneva declared that she felt like an icicle. Then they stood at the bonfire and talked to Phil D'Entremont and Avery Fry and even Sheriff Karl Barnes who had come out to keep an eye on things. It was warm and chilly and Phil had them all laughing with his jokes.

"I've got an idea," Stephen said to the group, out of earshot of Sheriff Barnes. "If you're game."

"What?" Clay asked him. "Since Avery spiked the cider, I'm game for anything." He put an arm around Geneva's shoulders.

Stephen really had a look in his eye. Brynn knew it from innumerable times with Boone and her cousins. It gave a little thrill of danger up her back, like prickling icicles. But, as Clay had said, the cider had been tampered with and when she looked at Geneva, she could tell that Geneva didn't mind a little danger, either.

"You," Stephen said to her very firmly. "don't worry. And we're going to see something you never saw in your life before. And if you're up to it, Clay, I got a challenge for you."

"I'm up to it," the other replied instantly. "Let's go."

"I do not want to go see your grandmother," Brynn said as they pulled up in Geneva's father's cutter just on the other side of Old Darcy's little stable. "I see her every day. That's enough for me."

"What're we doing here?" Clay asked.

Stephen jumped down into the snow and Brynn followed. "Come on," he told them, taking her hand. "You'll see. And we're not going anywhere near my grandmother."

The snow gave off a strange, blue-glow; almost a light of its own, and the moonlight made it all almost as bright as day. Stephen obviously knew his way around his grandmother's property very well, and he led the way to a small side door of the squat, brown building. Holding it open for the two girls, he ushered them all in and then pulled out matches and lit the lantern inside.

"Now, come over here and I'll show you," he said, going to the end of the stable, past the one horse in his stall to where what seemed to be a pile of blankets lay. Brynn had seen this stable more times than she wanted to count and she had never paid more than a passing glance to this side of the building. "You won't believe this," Stephen added as he began pulling back the cover.

It took him a minute or two to reveal what was underneath. It took up almost the width of the stable, small as it was, and what had appeared to be a pile of blankets was actually a long thickness of oilcloth. He rolled it back, Clay stepped forward to help, and when at last they moved aside and the lantern light revealed what it was, Brynn couldn't help a sharp intake of breath at the beauty of it.

It was a sleigh. It was a sleigh, but unlike any she had ever seen, for this was scrolled and carved and the whole length of the body was painted. Painted wasn't even exactly the word, either, she thought, for it was more than painted; it was a painting in itself. It was a mural that reached from bow to stern of the sleigh, rich with color and detail.

Clay took the lantern down from the hook where Stephen had hung it and held it closer. It was a mural of the self-same sleigh in the snow, drawn by a team of fine horses, spraying snow into the air as it approached a town over a hump-backed bridge. Every space of the side was filled with the scene and the realism was so complete, Geneva reached out one hand to touch the snowflakes.

"Oh my," Brynn heard herself say in a whisper.

"This is beautiful," Geneva said in a hushed voice.

"Yep," Stephen agreed. "My father said that my grandmother painted it herself."

"Oh my," Brynn repeated. "She did this?"

"Didn't know that about the old girl, did you?" Stephen grinned.

"Did you ever get to ride in it?" Geneva asked him.

"No," he replied. "But I'm going to tonight."

They all looked at him. In the lantern light, she had a flash of recognition. He looked a bit like Mrs. Darcy herself.

"You're not serious," Clay said.

"I sure am," Stephen told him. "Here, give me a hand. I remember when my father and uncles brought this over here. I was little, but I remember. This whole side of the barn slides, look, so that they could get it in." He was wrestling with the bolt as he was speaking, and with Clay's help and a small screek of protest from the long unused door, they managed to slide the panel back. Stephen was right; the whole side of the stable slid open, with the door that Brynn usually used to bring Angelina in and out as an inset, like the barns had at New House, in fact. She had never noticed.

"See," Stephen said in satisfaction, dusting his hands. "They backed it in. All we have to do is hitch the horses and it'll get pulled right out."

"What horses?" Geneva asked. She was always practical.

"Well," Stephen looked around. "Player here is as easy to drive as they come," he indicated the gelding in the only occupied stall. "He'll pull with anybody. Hitch him double with one of yours, Clay, and they'll handle it fine. And one will pull yours with no problem."

"They're Neeva's daddy's horses, and what makes you think I want to hand any of them over to you?" Clay asked.

Stephen looked at him. "Come on, McKenna," he said. "You're dying to and you know it."

Brynn could see, with a growing sense of alarm, that what Stephen said was true. "Clay, don't you dare," she said.

In ten minutes, she was seated beside Stephen in Mrs. Darcy's sleigh with the lap robe across her knees. Stephen chirped to the horses softly, his hands quiet on the lines, and they pulled the sleigh slowly out of the barn and across the snow under the fir trees. Behind them, Clay's cutter fell in behind them.

Brynn looked around them, at the snow covered trees with their limbs drooping, at the icy moonlight, at the leather upholstery, and tried to formulate in her mind what exactly it felt like. The whole feel of the sleigh was different, rich and big and heavy. Even the reins that Stephen held were thick and wide over the horses' backs. It slid over the snow in swishy silence. He smiled at her.

"Not bad, eh?" he said.

"I cannot believe you are doing this," she told him. "If your grandmother knew, you'd be a dead man."

"What she don't know won't hurt her a bit," he replied.

They pulled out on the road and turned toward town. Clay drove up beside them and said that they looked like a picture postcard. "Like one of those Currier and Ives things," was how he put it. There was nobody about and they had the road to themselves. Mrs. Darcy lived a bit out of town and there were few houses. There was no danger of them encountering anybody they knew, Brynn decided, beginning to relax. There was a warm wobbly feeling to everything. The boys talked back and forth, swapping barbs with one another, and she and Geneva talked.

After a bit, Geneva wanted to sit in the sleigh so Clay tied up his horse and they climbed in the second seat and they drove slowly up and back the little stretch of road some more. There was a slow curve that took them up to the last rise before town and they drove in a wide circle from the rise of the end of the curve before it came in sight of Mrs. Darcy's house.

Clay produced a small, suspicious bottle and everybody had a taste. Brynn thought it was nasty, but the warm feeling increased. They were all laughing and the horses plodded quietly and Stephen's shoulder was warm under her cheek. Geneva pointed under the trees and they saw three deer melting into the snowy forest. And then Stephen said:

"Oh, yes it could, too, Clay. You know it, too. That's why you scared to try." And Brynn knew she had missed something.

"Hellfire, I'm scared," Clay replied. "You're the one who should be scared. You want to make a wager? I'll wager you five bucks. This monstrosity won't make it up the rise, let alone win."

"That's what you think," Stephen said.

"Wager on what?" Brynn asked, sitting up.

"I'll make it ten," Stephen told him over his shoulder.

"Ten?" Clay asked.

"Unless you're scared."

"All right, ten it is," Clay said. "You got two horses, I got one. With your added weight, I'll even give you a head start. From the start to say, the tree nearest the road just over the rise. The big hemlock there. What say?"

"Do what now?" Brynn asked. "Don't tell me you two are…"

"Now, Brynnie, don't you worry your head about it," Clay told her. "It's between me and Steve. You and Neeva just go along for the ride."

"Go along where? What are the two of you up to?"

"They're just going to have a little race, Brynn," Geneva's face was excited. "It'll be fun. There's nobody about."

"What! Oh no you are not, Clay McKenna."

"Oh yes I am. Watch me," Clay vaulted out of the sleigh and handed Geneva out. "Come on, sweetie, we're going to whup some ass," he told her.

"Like hell you are," Stephen said.

"Stefan, don't do it," Brynn said to him. "If anything happens to this thing…"

"Nothing's going to happen," he assured her. "This is as stout as a steam engine. Can't nothing touch it. You just sit there and enjoy the ride."

Oh all right then, she thought. It'll be their funeral. The spirit of the thing was getting into her, anyway, as Clay lined up the Willis' little cutter with theirs. There was nothing she could have said to stop the two of them now, she knew, and suddenly with the moonlit snow stretching before them on the deserted road, the snow-laden trees pressing in, the horses shaking a jingle from their harness, she decided she didn't want to stop it, either. Clay and Stephen looked at each other, Geneva gave the word, and Stephen slapped the lines across the horses' backs with a yell.

Clay was as good as his word and let them have a good head-start. The horses leaped ahead in a startled gallop and Brynn clutched the seat as they did. Instantly, the wind that had been keen when they had been merely trotting along, was now whistling past in an icy slap, Stephen was standing like a chariot driver and the big sleigh was careening along at a great rate.

From behind them, as she looked back, she could see Clay begin whipping up his horse and the little cutter come racing after them. The trees blurred past them, the road disappeared beneath, and Brynn turned back to see the small hill become visible rising up out of the blue-white dark.

As they came pounding up at a fast approach, Clay pulled up alongside. She had barely time to see him before he gave out a rebel-yell of catastrophic proportions and their two horses shied away from him. In the space of a blink, the small cutter pulled ahead.

"Sonofabitch!" Stephen said in a businesslike way, slapping the lines again.

Clay got past them and Geneva turned to wave her handkerchief at them. "Whooo, Steve!" she yelled.

"You cheated, Clay!" Brynn yelled back.

They were all laughing, calling back and forth. It was glorious fun. The snow spray sounded like buckshot against the side, it flew stinging into their faces. Stephen moved up alongside again, then Clay would get ahead. Clay was standing now, legs braced wide, swaying with the cutter. They topped the rise neck and neck and the finish line was just in sight.

And then, in an instant, it was all over. As they topped the rise, there was buggy coming toward them.

Brynn only caught a glimpse of it as it floundered in the snow, coming slowly at a walk on the slippery surface. She caught a glimpse of the face of the driver under his hat, his eyes wide at the sight of them. She heard Stephen curse beside her and haul on the reins, heard Geneva scream and saw Clay jerk his horse the other direction, sending the cutter off the road and up the little slope around the buggy. Stephen sawed on the lines, pulling for all he was worth to get the sleigh over. There was a protesting sound of metal on hard ground and the sleigh began to tumble.

Brynn felt herself suddenly falling, falling, and the snow on the side of the road came up to meet her in wet cold softness. She hit full-faced into the snowbank and rolled over in time to see the mural painting hesitate above her, then groan its way over on top of her, blocking the sky. The horses were floundering near her, trying to keep their footing; she felt the ground shake when one fell.

The sleigh toppled slowly toward her. Something was pinning her legs. She grabbed her face and waited for the impact. There was an awful mixed up sound all around her, a thud of heaviness hit her and then silence.

"Dammit," Stephen scrambled up from where he had landed in his wild jump off the seat. The ground was iron hard frozen and his nose was bleeding, but he never noticed.

For a moment, he stood still, scarcely seeing the buggy's horse rearing nearby, it's driver cursing him for all he was worth. Moving aside, Stephen looked toward where Clay had pulled up and jumped down. The cutter had missed the buggy by inches, had managed to stay upright and had skidded to a stop at an odd angle twenty feet further on. Clay was running back toward them.

"Where's Brynnie!" he was shouting. "Steve, where's Brynnie!"

By the time Clay reached him, he had dodged around the tangle of harness, around the one horse wallowing in the ditch drift while the other was standing mercifully quiet, and was on his knees in the snow beside the overturned sleigh. It took him a moment or two to see her, for only her head and shoulders were visible, the sleigh covered the rest of her.

"Brynn!" he gasped and she swiveled her face around to see him. "Oh, God, Brynn! Are you hurt? What hurts?"

There was a trickle of blood at her mouth and down one side of her face, but she answered quite normally. "I'm all right," she told him calmly. "I'm stuck."

Clay's face appeared behind Stephen and he looked so horrified, Brynn was worried about him. "Oh, my God," he said. "Brynnie, honey…"

"It's all right, Clay," she replied. "I'm just stuck. I'm stuck under here."

"We got to get it off her," Stephen said. "Can you breathe? What hurts?"

"Nothing hurts," she insisted. "I'm just stuck."

"Look," Clay said. He was lying on his belly in the snow, digging at the snow beside her, peering up under the sleigh. "It's caught on something. It's up off her; it's not lying on her at all. Thank God. It's just…"

"My legs are stuck," she told them and wriggled around. "I can't get them out. What happened?"

"You wrecked us, that's what happened," Clay told her.

"I didn't do it. I wasn't driving."

"All right," Stephen said in his take charge way. He wiped blood off his face and looking about, went and got a fence rail. "Get another of these and we'll lift it off her."

"You got to do it easy." It was the driver of the buggy that spoke. His displeasure at them obviously put aside for the time being, he squatted in the snow to survey the situation. "Do it slow and easy and let her slip out from under if she can. Don't rush or you may drop it on her or it could slip off of whatever is holding it up there."

Clay looked down at her and she looked up at him and he could tell she was scared all of a sudden. He smiled and said: "Trust you to go getting yourself in a mess like this." And she smiled back at him.

"Ev'ybody jes hold still a minute," said the big voice and Clay saw Sherriff Barnes coming toward them in his tall boots. "Good God almighty, what the hell have you bunch done done to yourselves? That you, Jed?"

"Sure thing, Sherriff," the buggy driver turned toward him to say. "And t'warnt me, twas these young folks here that…"

Karl Barnes was a big bear of a man. He hustled by them all, took a look at Brynn on the ground and turning to Clay, ordered: "Cut those traces and get the horses out of here. They start bucking around, they make a mess of everything. Jed, go with the boy here and get the horses out."

Brynn lay still and commanded herself not to cry. The Sherriff came and squatted down next to her.

"You all right, miss?" he asked, not unkindly.

"Yessir," she replied.

"Well, we'll get you out in a minute," he told her patting her shoulder.

It was more than just a minute and she was shivering mightily by the time, with the help of the gathering crowd, the sleigh was levered off her legs and Clay and Barnes slid her out from under.

"Now jes stay still a minute, young lady," Karl Barnes said, kneeling next to her. "You other boys step on back and let me see to her. Give her some air. I know she's a pretty young lady, but she don't need all of you 'uns all around her."

Stephen came to her and stayed until Barnes pronounced that she could try to stand up if she wanted to. Then he and Clay helped her up and she hung onto Stephen as she limped out to the road. And then, she paused to take a look at the sleigh itself. Beside her, she heard Stephen sigh.

"Sure a mess," Barnes pronounced.

It was, true enough, a mess. Structurally, the sleigh seemed to be in one piece for it was, as Stephen had aptly stated, stout as a steam engine, but the mural on the side was half scraped away, with a huge caving-in along the whole of it, making the snow scene weirdly off-kilter. The scrollwork on one side was broken off, the heavy lines sawed asunder and Mrs. Darcy's horse had a limp.

"This yours, young feller?" Barnes asked Stephen.

"Sort of," he replied.

"Just how sort of is sort of?" the sheriff asked.

"It's a long story," Stephen told him.

Barnes faced him ponderously. "Boy," he said. "I got all the time in the world, but very little patience. You need to start talking. Clay McKenna," he added over his shoulder. "You let Miss Brynn sit in that cutter you were driving. She's shaking like a leaf. You two young ladies get warm; I need to talk to you two boys and Jed. Oh, Mr. Willis," he added as Geneva's father pulled up on his horse and jumped down, going to where Geneva stood crying. "Good. I'll need a statement from you, too. This other cutter is yours, am I right? Right, then. Let's get to the bottom of this."

-6-

Brynn answered the tap on her bedroom door and Boone put his head in.

"We're back," he told her unnecessarily.

She laid the book she had been trying to read across her knees. "Well?"

"Well what?"

"Come in here and tell me," she said irritably. "You took long enough."

Boone came in and looked toward the little heater standing unlit. It was cold as a tomb in there, but that just about figured, he thought. Brynn didn't allow any heaters lit upstairs, even when it was Brynn herself sick abed. Especially if it was Brynn herself, he supposed.

He came and sat on the foot of the bed. The girl sure looked a sight. There was a black and blue mark near one swollen eye that complimented the scrape down her face nicely.

"Your head still hurt?" he asked.

"Not too bad," she replied and he could tell she was lying. "So what happened?"

"You work for a helluva mean old lady, you know that?"

"Yes, I know. Do I still have my job or what?"

"Oh, you still have your job," he told her. "For the rest of your natural life, you have it. Till you pay off your share of four-hundred dollars, that is. I figure that'll be about fifty years."

"What!"

"And that only because Kevin went to bat for you with all the Kevin McKenna charm at his disposal. Oh, and

Steve's father put in a good word for you as well, I think. But it was Kevin that really saved the day."

"Oh, God," she put her face in her hands. "So how much do I owe the old bat then?" she asked, taking them away again.

"Hundred."

"Hundred! I wasn't even driving!"

"Yes, but you were there," Boone pointed out. "Kevin paid Clay's share up front, Willis paid Geneva's, Steve's father paid Steve's, but you get to pay yours all by yourself. Congratulations. Nice being head of a household, ain't it? She wanted your ass fired **and** you pay a hundred, but Steve's father pointed out that she'd never get her money if she did that, so she agreed to let you work it off. Thanks to Kevin."

"Oh, God," Brynn repeated. "But wait a minute," she added. "How will we live? I won't get any pay till I pay it off?"

Boone ran one hand through his hair. "Looks like about the size of it."

"But---that's impossible! We have to have that money. I have to get paid!"

"Don't look at me," he said. "You're the one who got in that stupid sleigh in the first place…"

"I know I know. Don't get started again." She had had quite enough of that conversation when she got taken home the evening before. It was, as she had pointed out to her brother, as if Boone had never done a bad thing in his life, the way he had carried on. Even looking as pathetic as she did and Sorrel being scared to death and crying over her hadn't stopped Boone.

"You need to go talk to Kevin," he said after a minute.

"What for?"

"What for? Well, for starters, you need to thank him for going out on a limb for you with the old bat. He really did do some slick talking for you, you know. And you need to go ask him for the money."

She stared at him. "What? For what money?"

"For a hundred dollars to pay Old Darcy. Then you're off the hook with her, you can get your regular wages, we pay back Kevin as we can, we can eat, everybody's happy. See?"

"Boone, I can't go ask Kevin for the money."

"Why not?"

"Because---because I can't. It's not his responsibility. We're supposed to be making it on our own…"

"We won't make it at all if you don't."

"I'm not asking Kevin for the money."

"Oh, yes you are."

"Oh, no I'm not."

"Then you're a fool," he told her. "And a stupid fool and all this about Old House and keeping the children together and being a family of Amy and Morgan's is a bunch of bullshit."

"It is not!"

"It is," he said and he was angry. "It's not about being a family at all if you don't. It's all about your pride. It's all about you and doing all this yourself and God forbid anybody help you. And you'd rather let Sorrel get sick and us not have nothing to eat and be cold as a witch's tit and in the end lose Old House and the children be split up anyway rather than ask Uncle Kevin for anything. Because it's all about you." He got to his feet off the bed. "You need to get your ass down to New House and talk to Kevin."

"You do it," she replied. "You want to so bad, you go down and ask him."

"No I will not," he told her. "You put yourself as head of this household…."

"Because no one else would do it!"

"….you need to go down there and thank Daddy's brother for going to bat for you up at Old Darcy's and ask him for help. It won't kill you. Part of being head of anything is knowing when to ask for help. And the time is now."

Brynn said nothing. She and Boone looked at each other a minute, then he added: "If you go down this afternoon, he can give you the bank draft for Old Darcy for Monday morning."

Kevin was at his desk and called: "Come," when the knock on the door came. A rather tentative knock it was and he half-wondered who it was for Janine never knocked like that. When the door opened, he knew why.

Brynn came in slowly, holding onto the knob as if she would scurry back out any moment. Kevin smiled at her. He knew that he should be thoroughly annoyed with the girl, every bit as annoyed as he was with his son Clay when he had been told about the fiasco, but he couldn't, somehow.

Annoyed wasn't exactly the word to describe how he had been at Clay. He had wished mightily that he could still take off his belt with the boy, but, at eighteen, he was a little too old for that. But he could give him a piece of his mind, which he had done for a good long while as they had ridden to Mrs. Darcy's house earlier that day. He had figured that, since Boone had been along as Brynn's representative, he had relayed Kevin's displeasure to the girl. Kevin hadn't expected to see her any time soon.

"Brynnlin," he said. "come on in. And sit down. I thought you weren't supposed to be out of bed today."

She came in and shut the door behind her. "I'm all right," she replied, coming to sit at the chair he indicated. "I was tired of staying in bed."

He looked at her keenly. She certainly didn't look too chipper. Her one eye was black and swollen, the scrape down her face was turning several different colors and there was a neat split at the corner of one lip. She winced when she sat and hugged her arms about herself.

"I needed to talk to you, Uncle," she said.

"All right," he replied, settling back in his chair.

She was looking everywhere but at him. "Uncle Kevin," she said. "Thank you. For going over to Mrs. Darcy's and all. Boone told me that you helped save my job. Thanks."

"You don't have to thank me," Kevin replied. "After all, it my fool son who thought it all up."

"Not exactly," Brynn told him. "It was Stefan who showed us the sleigh. And he wanted to race as much as Clay did."

"Well, from what I hear, Clay was the one who thought up the race in the first place. With Willis' cutter and horses no less."

"Well, yessir, I guess so," she admitted.

"Which don't mean that the rest of you had to be a bunch of sheep and go along with it."

"No, sir, I know."

"You could've got yourselves killed, you know. Damn near did, from what I hear; that sleigh landing on top of you."

"Yes, sir."

"Sherriff Barnes said there was liquor in the mix, too. That true?"

"Yes, sir," she toyed with the end of her scarf, not looking at him.

"You have some, did you?"

"Well, yes, sir," she said.

"That wasn't too smart, either, was it? And what do you think your Mama would've thought of that? Off drinking with a boy and then all the rest of it?"

She swallowed and said: "She wouldn't have liked it, that's for sure." She looked at him then and added: "I'm sorry, Uncle Kevin. Truly. I am."

"Well." He sighed, looking at her. "I'm sorry, too," he said. "Seems like I should have stopped it, somehow. Since your Mama and Daddy---well, you lot are sort of my responsibility, you know. If I'd been doing my job, maybe you wouldn't have gotten into all that."

"Oh, no Uncle," she told him. "It wasn't your job. You didn't have any responsibility about it. It was our fault, all of it. Not yours."

She had her Mama's eyes. Amy's eyes in Morgan's face; but Morgan wouldn't have sat there so contrite. Morgan would've owned up to it, but he would have done it in such a way, that everyone would have known that he thought it was worth it. A little like Clay had done, actually, Kevin realized in resignation.

"Uncle Kevin?" she said.

"Yes, honey."

"I need to ask you a favor," she said. "I wish I didn't, but I do. And if you don't want to, I don't blame you a bit. I really don't."

"All right," he replied. "What is it?"

She looked for all the world as if she was in front of a firing squad, he thought. All beat up and scared and a little defiant. Her daddy would have moved heaven and earth not to have her look like that.

"Could you---would you lend us the hundred dollars to pay old, er, Mrs. Darcy?"

"Of course."

"I know it's a lot of money. A whole lot of money. And I know I don't deserve you to do it, cause I made all that ruckus about Old House and taking the children back and trying to be grown up and all…"

"It's all right. Of course you can have the money."

She stopped and looked at him. "Sir?"

"Of course you can have the money," he repeated. "Actually, if you hadn't come down, I was going to walk up and bring you a bank draft after a little bit."

"You were?"

"Well, you can't work for Mrs. Darcy for no wages, can you? You'd be an indentured servant to her for years at that rate."

"Yes, sir. You---you were already going to give it to me?"

Kevin leaned forward in his chair. "Brynnlin," he said, looking right at her. "I want you and Boone and the children to keep on doing what you're doing."

"You do?"

"Yes! What did you think? That I'm sitting down here waiting for you to fail?"

She didn't answer.

"Brynnie! Is that what you think? Is that what you think I want---for you bunch up there to fail at it and have to come crawling back down to us?"

"Well," she said and hesitated. "I guess not, not really."

"Of course not really," he told her.

Brynn could see he meant it. She thought her uncle was a very handsome man; nearly as handsome as her daddy had been. She knew that Kevin and her mother had been "thick as thieves" as her daddy put it and that, when they were growing up, they had been the ones who got up to no good and got in trouble and played pranks together.

She even recalled that her uncle had helped her mother "borrow" their brother, Jim's horse to run in a race and how, when her mother had won and Jim had found out, how they both had been in all sorts of trouble for awhile. She hazarded a look at her uncle now, at him settled back again in his chair, searching for his matches, and saw that she had hurt him somehow.

She reached forward to the little box and handed him a match with a smile. She knew how her smile affected people, especially her uncle. "I'm sorry, Kev," she said, using her mother's name for him. "I guess I never really thought about it, about how you felt about us doing Old

House and all. I guess maybe it was just convenient to think you didn't like it."

He took the match and picked up his pipe. "Well, I do like it," he told her. "I worry about you up there, and your aunt Janny would just as soon the children were down here where she could play mother duck to them, but we're both damn proud of you. So," he pulled forth the big bank book from its drawer and swung it open. "Let's get down to business."

She was so relieved and so ready to get out of there, she had closed the study door and was dashing down toward the side door to avoid seeing Janine, not looking where she was going and ran slap into him at the dark corner of the hall. She nearly fell over him, actually, and he steadied her and when she looked up to see who it was, her heart flipped over itself. It was Adam.

"Whoa, girl," he said, setting her on her feet again. "Where's the fire?"

"Oh, I'm sorry," she replied. "I'm just---," she looked over her shoulder furtively. "---just was trying to not see your mother, actually," she admitted. She wound her muffler about her neck. She hadn't been this close to Adam in awhile. She wished he didn't get her so mixed up, and smell so good and look so---right.

He grinned and that made it even worse. "So'm I, to be honest," he told her. "I'm sneaking in to see my father."

"That's where I was, just now," she said. "He's in the study."

He looked down at her, seeing her in the dusky light. "Are you all right, by the way?" he asked. "I heard what happened last night. That fool brother of mine. Are you all right? You've got a black eye, haven't you?"

"I'm fine," she said and, because he reached out to touch her face where the bruise was, she stepped back a little. "And it wasn't all Clay's fault. We were all in on it. It was sort of fun, for a little while."

"Yes, I remember that kind of fun," he replied.

They were silent a moment, an awkward moment, then Adam added: "I was going to look you up after awhile, anyway. After I talked with Pa. I have something to tell him, then I was going to come tell you. You saved me a trip."

"What is it?" she asked. Something about his voice was strange.

"Got a letter from Bethy," he said. "She says she's divorcing me."

Brynn felt her mouth drop open. "Di-divorce?"

"So she says. And I believe her."

He was holding his gloves and fiddling with them, not meeting her eyes.

"Well, could you---couldn't you stop her?"

"I don't want to stop her," he said and then looked her straight in the eye.

"Oh."

"That's what she wants me to do, of course," he went on. "She wants me to beg and cry and convince her not to, go racing up there to Missouri and drag her back. But, I'm sick of all that. I ain't doing it any more. I've done that enough, all the other times. I'm done with that."

There was a sound from the back of the house, from the kitchen and they both looked toward it as if afraid of being seen together.

"What about Gidyun?" Brynn asked. Adam always liked the way she said his name.

"She can't keep me away from my son," he replied and she could tell that he had thought about all that. "She won't dare try. But, well, he needs his mother now. He's too little to be away from her. We'll just have to work out something until he's old enough to come back to live here with me." His mouth was very set and grim. "He'll be back here with me as soon as he's old enough."

She watched him, looking so different than he used to be. He used to be the one who was always laughing, making Boone laugh, even more than Clay did now. He hadn't been that way in a long time. Now he was looking past her. He had lived a different life from any of the rest of them for a long time. She took her gloves out of her coat pocket and began putting them on so she wouldn't have to see his face.

"I wanted to tell you; to have you hear it from me," he said.

She looked back up at him and asked him: "Why?"

He shrugged. "I guess to see your reaction, maybe. I don't know."

"Why?" she repeated. "What difference does it make what I think? You didn't care what I thought when you married her, what difference should it make now?"

There now, she thought at his expression. You want to talk about it, we'll talk.

"I did care what you thought," he said.

"No, you didn't."

"Yes, I did," he insisted. "I cared too much. That was the problem. That's always been the problem."

"Yes, it has, hasn't it," she agreed. "And so now what? What would you have me do?"

He sighed. "Brynnie," he said. "Just don't---don't turn on me. That's all. The rest of them, they never understood."

"And I do?"

He was silent and then repeated: "Just don't turn on me."

"I'll never do that," she said. "and you know it."

He went on past her then, and left her there, but as he passed, he put one hand on her arm for a moment. She felt the warmth of his hand there almost all the way home even through the cold.

As Katie came in the back door of Old House, she was surprised to see Brynn at the stove. She didn't knock, as was the custom, and so was also a bit taken aback at her sister's expression when she saw who it was. It was evident that Katie was not the person that Brynn most wanted to see at that moment.

"Oh," Brynn said. "Hello."

"Brynnie, what in the world," Katie replied, setting the big basket she carried on the kitchen table. "Come here, baby," she added to little Amelia who was staggering around in the layers of clothing in which her mother had bundled her against the cold. "Let me take your things off. Brynnie, I thought you were supposed to be in bed. I brought some supper up for all of you. Hold still, Amelia. I'll have you undone in a second."

"Oh," Brynn repeated. "So you heard about it, then."

Katie sat down in the nearest chair and unwound the scarf from about her daughter's neck. "Heard about it?" she said. "Yes, you could say that. Buck heard from his father about Clay's escapade that nearly got you killed."

Brynn went on stirring the pot, one hand on her hip, and didn't disillusion her. If Clay wanted to take the blame for it, she had done her duty explaining to Uncle Kevin. She decided she would let Katie think what she wanted to.

Kate was sitting, bent over double taking Amelia's things off, and she looked up at her sister from her upside down position, her eyes very blue under her blue hat. "Are you all right, then?" she asked and Brynn's conscience smote her a little. Kate was so genuinely concerned about her.

"Yes, I'm all right," she replied. "Do you want some coffee? Or the water's hot for tea."

"You sit," Kate commanded, hanging Amelia's coat and hat and scarf on the hook on the door and taking off her own coat. "I'll get my own. You sure you're all right? You don't too all right to me."

"Thanks," Brynn a bit dryly, fingering her eye. "It does look a bit gruesome, doesn't it."

Her sister came and took her shoulders in her hands, turning her to face her and examining her critically as she used to do when she was a little girl. "It looks like you've been in a fight," she told her. "It looks like it hurts, that's what it looks like." Releasing her, she went to the table in her businesslike way and began unpacking the basket she had brought. "But, aside from that, did you have a good time with that Stephen Darcy fellow?"

Amelia toddled over to Brynn who set the spoon aside and scooped her up into her arms. Amelia smiled all over her little face. She was a spunky little thing with curly blonde hair some several shades darker than her mother's and brown eyes. Brynn kissed her and replied:

"Stefan? Yes, I had a good time with him, I guess. Actually, yes, I did have a good time."

"He's a nice looking fellow," Kate said. "Dark, isn't he? Seems friendly."

"Yes, he's nice," Brynn replied. "He's just not..."

She stopped abruptly and Kate looked at her. "Not Adam McKenna, though, is he?" she finished for her. Brynn glanced at her warily, but her sister's expression was kind.

"No, he's not Adam," she agreed with a sigh.

"Believe me, I know how you feel," Kate said. "Those McKenna laddies; they're hard to resist. Listen, I'll put this stuff in your larder and you do whatever you want to with it. I brought half a layer cake; thought Jimbo would be tickled with that."

"Thanks."

"You don't mind, do you?" she asked from the pantry and stuck her head out. "Just wanted to give you a breather, if you needed it."

Brynn went to the table and sat down with her niece on her lap. Amelia immediately wriggled and got down, waddling off on her fat legs. "I do need a breather," she admitted. "I'm tired."

"I know you are," her sister said. "Where is everybody?"

"I don't know," she said wearily. "They're around somewhere. You brought butter, too?" she added, brightening. "Oh, Sister. We haven't had butter in ages."

"Well, for Pete's sake, why didn't you tell me?" Katie said briskly, bustling from the pantry to the stove and peeping into the soup pot. "Don't you know that Mama always shared the milk with Janny and me? Whoever was churning passed butter and buttermilk around, then next time there was more milk than the other could have use for, they sent it to the next house and so on. We can do that again. Just get Jimbo to take the milk down the hill to my place every so often and I'll churn some up for you and keep some cream or whatever for me. You don't have time for all that."

Brynn suddenly felt an overwhelming surge of warmth toward her bossy, take-charge older sister. They went on talking about chores and Brynn's work while Amelia toddled around chasing the cat, and Kate seasoned the soup in that way she had. Brynn had always admired the way her sister had with cooking; she couldn't quite get it right.

She said as much to Kate and Kate laughed at her. You should have seen some of the concoctions she tried to make Buck eat when they were first married, she told her. Brynn hadn't heard about any of that. Kate said that she had been a bit young to pay attention to when she would be crying to Amy about her newlywed trials.

"You and Buck had trials? I can hardly believe that," Brynn told her. "Oh, Melia, honey, don't pull Tommycat's tail. She doesn't like it."

"Oh, Buck and I had our share," Katie said. "This soup's about done. Want me to pull it off the heat?"

"I don't care," Brynn replied. "You mean, you and Bucko had fights and all that?"

"Oh, yes," Kate laughed. "Let me tell you…"

By the time Sorrel and Jerusha came in, followed soon thereafter by Jordan and lastly, Boone, Brynn had to look twice at the clock. She was holding Amelia who had fallen fast asleep on her lap as they talked, and it was nearly five-thirty.

"And I need to be going," Katie said, washing up the last of the dishes. Jordan was already slicing up the new bread and setting it to toast and Sorrel was plundering the pantry. "Don't eat all that at once, Shrimp," she added to her. "And you girls wash up for your sister. She needs to go on to bed early. Bye, Bernie," she said, dropping a kiss on the top of her head and gathering up her daughter. "Don't forget about the churning."

When she had gone, Boone said quietly as he was ladling out the soup into bowls: "Seems like Kate came in handy today."

"Yes, she did," Brynn replied.

"She would more often if you'd let her," he added.

"Well," Janine said that evening, climbing into bed beside Kevin. "There you are, you see."

Kevin looked at her. "Yes, here I am. What does that mean?"

Of course he knew what it meant. He wished he didn't, or that he could ignore her and it and go to sleep, for it had been a long day, but he had lived with the woman beside him for a long time and he knew that that wish was an impossibility.

"You know what I mean," she replied. She had lived with him a good while, too. "There you are. Men. Men and their dissatisfaction. And our son is one of them."

"Meaning Adam?"

"Yes, meaning Adam! Who else? Here he has a wife and a little boy and a job and enough family to beat the band and a home and everything and he runs her off."

Kevin set his book down and replied: "Well, he **had** a wife, of a sort."

"What do you mean by that?"

"I mean," he said. "She's a first class ninny and you and everyone else knows it. Personally, I don't know how he's put up with her this long."

"Which he should have taken into consideration before he went jumping into bed with her down in Duggansville and getting her pregnant," Janine said tartly.

"I agree," her husband agreed. "But he didn't. Any more than you or I did, may I remind you."

"Yes, but that was a different kettle of fish, too."

"It certainly was," he said.

They looked at each other. He looked at her auburn eyes so close to his and she looked about as annoyed as he was. So he took a deep breath and added: "I was wildly in love with you, if I remember. Almost as much as I am now. Adam wasn't. And isn't. Maybe he wants something more."

"He wants something different," she replied. "That doesn't necessarily mean more."

"And by that, I presume you mean..."

"Will you stop being so obtuse!"

"Obtuse?"

"I mean what I mean. And what I mean is Rebecca Brynn McKenna, that brother of yours' daughter up the hill."

"Yes, I know exactly who you mean."

"Then why didn't you say so?"

"I was hoping that you would think how that would sound and not say it."

"It's true, whether I say it or not."

"Yes, I know it's true," Kevin admitted with a sigh. "I just wish it wasn't."

"So do I."

"And the way you talk about her---it's like she's the other woman. It's Brynnlin we're talking about, you know. Our Brynnie."

Janine was silent, and then, because she saw the look in his eyes, she snuggled down next to him and put her cheek against his shoulder. "Yes, I know it's our Brynnie," she said in a different tone. "And you know how much I love the girl. Like she was my own. She practically is, if it comes to that. I helped raise her, like Amy raised ours. How could I keep from loving her? How could Adam keep from loving her, really?"

"You talk like she's the enemy," Kevin pointed out.

"She's too much like that brother of yours. She's Morgan McKenna all over again, in a body that a man would kill for."

"If you want to see Morgan McKenna, look at Boone," Kevin told her.

"Boone may look like him, but he's Amy through and through," Janine replied. "Brynn----she's tough. She gets a look about her---oh, I don't know. And that fool son of ours can't leave well enough alone. Why can't he just be content? He made his bed, why can't he just stay in it?"

"Like you did?"

She looked up at him from her cozy position. "I never was tempted to stay anywhere else," she said simply. "And that's the truth."

He smiled at her. "Me neither. And that's the truth, too."

Going back to Mrs. Darcy's was hard. It was even harder than Brynn had expected, and she had in no means been looking forward to it. But, on that first day, the Monday after the disastrous Friday night of the party, when she had resolutely stabled Angelina without looking too hard at the sleigh back in its proper place, she very nearly saddled her right back up and rode away. Her eye was still swollen, the scrape down her face, although not so angry red, was now scabbed over which was worse, and every muscle in her body ached in ways that seemed unreasonable. There were new bruises here and there, which fortunately didn't show, but which made her wince when she moved, and all in all, she figured she wasn't fit to look at. On the other hand, she decided as she forced herself to walk to the little house, maybe Mrs. Darcy would take pity on her, at least a little.

The snow had pretty much melted, as it usually did in the Georgia hills after the first couple of days. It was one of the things that her daddy had liked the best about living here; he didn't love the snow like her mama had done. A little was enough for him, then a quick thaw and back to just winter. Until the next time, which usually came after a few weeks, then back to melt again. For now, there were patches of dreary snow in shaded places, wet dead leaves and no sunshine to help the feel of the place. Brynn marched herself up to the kitchen door and in before she thought too much about it.

Rosemary turned from the biscuits she was cutting out and her face betrayed how the girl looked, although she said nothing, of course.

"Good morning," Brynn said and the tall woman nodded.

"Has Mrs. Darcy had breakfast this morning yet?" she asked.

Rosemary indicated the biscuits on the table before her.

Brynn sighed. The old lady was always in a better mood if she had had breakfast before she arrived. The fact that she hadn't usually meant that she had slept late, which usually meant that she had had a bad night with her lumbago, which usually---or almost usually---meant that she would not be in a pleasant mood to begin with. Not that she ever was in a pleasant mood, Brynn thought rather savagely. She took off her things, hung them in resignation, and went to face her.

"Well, you decided to bring yourself to work, did you?" Mrs. Darcy greeted her.

"Yessum."

"And don't say 'yessum'. I have told you before. I'm not a possum to be addressed such."

"Yes, ma'am. Mrs. Darcy..."

"You decided to come yourself today, I see, rather than hide behind your uncle and brother, did you?"

"Yes, ma'am. Mrs. Darcy, I just wanted to say..."

"Your uncle did some fine talking for you," she went on. "Fine talking for you and about you, not that I've seen any evidence of all the attributes that he said you have. And your brother spoke up for you, too."

Brynn blinked. "He did?"

"Yes. Even he seemed to think it was worth his while to come to see me himself, not hide in bed."

"Yes, ma'am. But the doctor said I shouldn't get up out of bed, otherwise I would have..."

"Doctor? Where did you get money to pay for a doctor to go see you?"

"We didn't. I mean, he came by and saw me and told us not to worry about it."

"Charity," Mrs. Darcy pronounced. "And then, if he said not to worry about it, then you weren't that bad off to begin with. He charges me a pretty penny, I can tell you that, whenever he comes out to say he can't do anything about my lumbago. If he didn't think it was worth charging money, there are only two reasons—either you were shamming the whole time because you wanted sympathy, or it's pure charity. Which was it?"

Brynn thought about that a minute. "I guess I was scared to come see you, ma'am."

The old lady gave a grim smile. "Preferable to charity, eh?"

"Mrs. Darcy," Brynn said doggedly. "I just want to say that I'm very sorry for what happened."

"For what happened?" she echoed. "For what happened? As if it was an earthquake or a hail storm. An act of God, was it? It didn't just happen---you and that wretched fool of a grandson did it! You did it, it didn't just happen."

"Yes, ma'am, that's true. And I'm truly sorry."

"I'm sure you are. Now. You weren't sorry when it was going on, however, were you? Well? Were you?"

Brynn looked at the fire burning brightly and considered, then decided that it wasn't worth it. "No, ma'am," she replied.

Again that dry, grim smile. "Good answer," she replied. "And your half-hearted apology is duly noted, but not necessarily accepted. Now, you may go bring me my heavier afghan and my tonic. I need a dose before breakfast what with all this fol-der-rol."

"Yes, ma'am." She turned to go, then Mrs. Darcy added:

"That grandson of mine been out to see you since? Or has he decided you aren't worth the trouble?"

"Yes, ma'am, he has," Brynn replied.

"Bringing flowers and tea and sympathy, no doubt," she said.

"Yes, ma'am," Brynn replied. She didn't want to tell the details, anyway.

"Well," Mrs. Darcy said. "I'll give him that, anyway."

Brynn took the opportunity and left to get the tonic. The fact was that Stephen had been out to Old House early on Saturday morning, so early that Boone and Sorrel were still struggling with making the oatmeal for breakfast.

Brynn herself hadn't been allowed up yet and Stephen's appearance at her bedroom door with a rather odd bouquet of holly tied with ribbon was quite a surprise. He had driven her home the night before, of course, after Barnes got finished with them and the doctor had looked her over right on the spot, but she had only wanted to get inside and into bed. She scarcely remembered it.

Stephen had been truly horrified about the whole thing, Brynn could tell. She had accepted the holly, accepted his apology—again—and allowed him to kiss her battered cheek while she sat in her bed; knowing all the while that her mother would have thoroughly disapproved. Her daddy would have never let him in the door, if it came to that, she figured.

And somewhere in the midst of the incident, Brynn had come to really like Stephen Darcy. They had connected, somehow, though not in the way that she and Adam were (because they had always been connected) or in the way she had with Jackson Flynn. The way with Jackson was the rather thunderbolt variety; it didn't compare. But she had decided that she liked Stephen, despite the black eye he had given her.

She trotted into the kitchen again, out of breath with the haste of her retreat, and Rosemary gave her a sympathetic look as she handed her down the tonic bottle and tumbler. She trotted back to the front room, remembering to give Mrs. Darcy the bank draft from Kevin.

The rest of the day consisted of her enduring more of the same lecture and inquisition and managing to survive. By the evening, she was tired and achy and dreading the long ride home only to have to preside over one of Jerusha's suppers. Life was bleak.

Well, at least I'm not indentured to her any more, she reminded herself. At least I will get paid. But it was all she could do to even feel grateful for that.

"Good-evening, Miss Carson."
"Good-evening, Mr. McKenna. Good to see you again."
"And, it's good to see you, Miss Carson," he told her.
They stood and looked at each other, smiling, and then she added: "Won't you come in?"
"I am in," he replied, and looked over his shoulder at Ginny, who had answered his ring at the big front door and was now standing observing the little exchange with interest.

Schuyler looked flustered, blushed a little, and said: "Then won't you come into the parlor? Dinner isn't quite ready."

Boone offered her his arm and she took it. If he didn't look so delicious, she could probably catch her breath and act more like herself. But the fact was that Boone---as his sisters would have put it---"cleaned up pretty good", and the transformation from his work clothes was rather spectacular.

There hadn't been a McKenna male born who didn't look superb in white shirt, black tie and jacket, and the fact that it was Boone's one good suit and had been his one good suit for several years now, made no difference to the effect it had on people. It certainly was having an effect on Schuyler.

Boone, too, was thinking that Schuyler was particularly beautiful this evening. The dress she wore was by no means her only dinner frock, or the best dinner frock she owned, but it was a satiny dark blue that set off the color of her eyes and dipped demurely at the neckline, showing creamy skin in contrast to the near-black of her hair. Her hair itself was coiled close to the back of her head, thick and shining, and Boone wanted more than anything, to unpin it and have it fall over his hands. Instead, he looked down at her face from his superior height and said quietly:

"Are we going to be this formal all evening?"

He had such dark eyes, she was thinking. Such dark eyes and those lashes that any woman would wish for herself. "It's just a bit different from the last time," she replied. "Isn't it? A bit different from sitting on the floor playing canasta." Which was what they had done the week before, the Friday of Geneva Willis' party.

When Boone had asked Sam Carson if he could call on his daughter, they had both known that it would have meant that they would be sitting in the Carson front parlor, for Boone had no means to come drive them anywhere, even for a Sunday afternoon.

So, he had come and knocked on her front door that Friday evening and they had sat by the fire, albeit not in the front parlor, but in the library across the hall. There in the dark paneled room with the bookcases reaching to the ceiling, they had sat on the hearth rug and they had both ended up laughing so hard at nothing as they played cards, her mother had poked her head in.

"Aren't you scared?" she asked him now, seeing his amusement.

"Of?"

"Of having dinner with the boss. And the boss's wife. Not to mention the boss's sons who are heirs to the throne. Doesn't that intimidate you a little?"

"Should it?"

"Do you always answer a question with a question?" she asked, in mild irritation.

"Do I?" he replied and laughed at her.

"I thought I heard voices," came the booming voice from the hall and Sam Carson came striding in, looking, his daughter thought with pride, stately and handsome in his own right in his dinner jacket. "There you are, daughter," he added. "McKenna, good evening."

"Good evening, sir," Boone stepped to take his extended hand.

"Nice to have you here," Sam told him, wrestling with his cuff button. "Goddammit, can you get this, Sky?"

"Don't curse, Papa," Schuyler came forward to help him. "At least not in front of company."

"Company," her father snorted. "I just seen the boy two hours ago. And he's heard me say a helluva lot worse than that, ain't that right, McKenna."

"Yes, sir," Boone replied.

"Hate these damn buttons," the big man continued. "Hate this dressing for dinner, if it comes to that. Want a cigar, McKenna? Always have one before dinner. Have one after dinner, too."

"Thank you," Boone said.

"Yes, hate all this dressing up every time you turn around," he went to the carved cigar box on the mantle, pulled forth two and clipped the ends before handing Boone one. "But, the wife decides what goes inside this house. I decide what goes on outside. That's the deal," he struck his match, puffed until the end glowed, then handed the match to Boone. "You and your wife need to get all that straight between you before you marry," he added, spewing smoke toward the ceiling and pointing his cigar at him. "See that you do that before you and Sky get hitched."

"Papa!" Schuyler said in astonishment.

"Mr. Carson," Esther Carson said, coming into the room at that moment. "Dinner is ready. Oh, good evening," she added in a somewhat different tone. "Schuyler, you may show your guest to dinner."

Mrs. Carson was a regally dressed matron; the pearl choker she wore made her more so; the look on her face and the sweep of her skirts had intimidated quite a few young men. As she turned and left, Schuyler came and put her hand through Boone's arm again saying with a grin:

"You may come to dinner, now, Mr. McKenna."

"Stay and finish your cigar," Sam ordered, leaning an elbow on the mantle. "I am. I want to hear what you found out down at the slough when you and Comfort went to check that end of the fence. And you need to think about going with Cale up to the north end of the property and look at the fence up near the shack..."

"Papa, don't let's talk work all evening," Schuyler pleaded.

"I won't talk it all evening," her father told her. "But there're things that need to be discussed and we will discuss them before we go in to the table so I won't have to hear from your mother about not talking about it at dinner. So, McKenna?"

They didn't talk work all evening, it was true. But they talked enough about it that it carried them in to the dining room and well into the first course, with Cale and Seth adding to it. It carried on so long that Esther did have to gently remind her husband that it was not dinner conversation, but even so, Sam ignored her suggestion until he had been satisfied with Boone's and his sons' answers.

"I know that top of the property fence is in need of attention," he said at last. "It'll be a day or two's worth of work what with travel time there and back. Got damn too much land, that's the problem. Just as soon sell some of it as try to keep up with it, except that probably some damn snob gentlemen farmer'd probably buy it and put up some damn summer house like they got over in Habersham County. Then all we'd have is dinner parties and traveling around from pillar to post to satisfy the neighbors. By the way," he added to his wife. "When's that damn dinner party you're so all fire set on? Don't tell me it's this week?"

Esther patted her mouth with her napkin. "You know perfectly well it is next Saturday," she replied. "And I do hope, Seth that the muss from the ceiling being repaired will be taken care of by then. Mister McKenna," she said with a suddenly brightening. "Perhaps you could be so kind during the first of the week to sweep up the plaster that has fallen."

"Mother," Schuyler began, but her father interrupted.

"Good God, Essie," he said. "The man's not a cleaning woman! Get Ginny or one of the maids to do it. I got better things for McKenna to do. You and Seth need to go up to the north woods and do that fencing like I was talking about. Don't worry, Seth," he said at his son's expression. "You'll be back by Saturday night. Is the Governor coming, did you say, Essie?"

Schuyler's mother sat a little straighter. Her back never touched any chair, but at Sam's words, she squared her thin shoulders. "Yes, he and his wife as well as Congressman Hadley and his wife. Mister Carson, you must make sure we have the proper boys to take charge of the horses this time. No white boys, it just doesn't look right. These hill boys with their accents, it's not the thing. Comfort needs to be in charge…"

"Comfort's just a kid," Sam told her.

"These hill boys," Esther said. "All they know about is mules. They shouldn't be handling the carriage horses. Don't you think so, Mister McKenna?" she asked, turning toward him with her bright birdy eyes.

Boone set down his wine glass and said: "I'm not sure that I'm the one to be asking, Mrs. Carson, since I am one of those hill boys."

"Oh, but you're different," Esther said. "You're people are New Orleans, are they not?"

"Yes, ma'am, but not for awhile," he replied. "My grandfather moved to Missouri right after the war. My mother and father were both born there, but we've been here since I was twelve. And as for handling horses, anybody who can handle a jack stock mule can deal with any horse. My uncle's mules are smarter and meaner than any horse I know. Any man, or boy, who can get them to cooperate can take full charge of a horse."

Schuyler's mother turned eyes front again and replied: "Well, be that as it may, it doesn't look correct for a white boy to be handling the horses."

"And God forbid that we look incorrect when the Governor comes to call," Sam agreed, draining his glass. "I'm sure he'd be quite flabbergasted to have a white boy take his horse to the barn."

"The carriage house, Mister Carson," Esther amended gently.

Boone looked across at Schuyler with the same amused look as her father, she was grateful to see. The rest of the meal was spent in relatively congenial conversation. Cook had done the roast beef proud, as usual, and had Schuyler but known it, Boone had not had such a dinner in many a month.

He kept wishing it would be proper to ask for any of the food left over to take home to the mouths as Old House, especially when he saw the serving dishes still half full at the end of the meal. The hot roasted potatoes, done just the way Jordan liked them, especially took his eye. He couldn't help sighing a little when the maid lifted them away and then the dessert was brought in.

"Oh, good," Sam said, sitting well back in his chair at the head of the table. "None of that fancy blank-mange stuff tonight."

"I asked for this special," Schuyler said as the huge layer cake was brought in and set before Esther. "You said you liked chocolate, Boone."

"I do," he replied. "I haven't had any in a long time."

"Well, company gets the first piece," Esther said in a burst of hospitality, slicing into the icing.

"I've always heard that the Irish are partial to bread pudding," Cale said, rolling his glass between his fingers. "You are Irish, McKenna?"

"Mostly," Boone replied.

"And the rest of you?"

"Good God, you want his pedigree?" Sam asked. "If you want mine, too, I can tell you that I'm half-Irish, too. So that makes you a quarter, remember. And on your mother's side…"

"That'll do, Mister Carson," Esther said, passing the plate of thick-sliced cake to Boone. "I don't think that is quite dinner conversation, if you please."

"No, I don't quite, either," Sam agreed with a wink in Boone's direction. "Your side of the family would spoil anybody's appetite."

Afterward, when Sam and his sons had retired to the billiard room for brandy and cigars, Schuyler instead insisted that she show Boone the library. Sam grumbled that she had shown him the library last time he came to call, if he remembered right; but Schuyler replied that after all Boone had come to see her, not to wile away the evening with her father and brothers.

"So," Boone said when they had withdrawn to the large, dark-paneled room, Schuyler's hand tucked into his arm. "How did I do?"

She looked up at him inquiringly and he was smiling. "Well," she replied. "as far as Papa is concerned, you could've danced on the table. He likes you."

"And the rest of them?"

"That remains to be seen."

"That's what I figured."

"And as for me," she added. "I think you did just fine."

"Well, good," he told her. "I enjoyed myself."

Boone had decided that he really liked the library. He liked the high glassed bookshelves, the way the carved dowels near the ceiling threw shadows, the scent of old print and leather. In the center of the room was a large, felt-topped table, set about with holders for pens, ink wells in curious shapes, and a few books strategically placed.

From what Boone could tell, neither Sam nor either of his sons used the room for what it was intended, or even ventured in much at all. Schuyler read a book from time to time, but, like much about the Big House, this room was an orderly show with Esther's touch everywhere. Boone, however, liked looking at the titles in the bookcases and wished briefly that he could sit at the big table with one of the ornate, gold-embossed books, especially on a cold night with a fire in the fireplace, as it was now.

"You're invited, you know," Schuyler said.

Boone turned from his examination of titles in the far case and looked at her. She was standing with her hands behind her back and the firelight was doing nice things to her skin.

"To what?" he asked.

"To what?" she echoed. "Weren't you at dinner with me? You couldn't have missed my mother's favorite topic of conversation. To her party next week, of course."

"I'm invited?"

"Yes," she said. "As my guest."

Boone smiled a little. "No, I don't think so."

"Why not?"

He opened the bookcase carefully, swinging it open on silent hinges, and took out the book he had found. It wasn't one of the stately, tooled-leather bound ones; the cover was old and worn and, when he opened it, the binding was coming apart. He turned to the inside cover and read the inscription.

"Boone," she said. "Why not?"

He closed the book back gently, replaced it into its place, and swung the door closed again. He turned to face her. "I'll probably be working," he replied.

"Not if I invite you," she said. "Papa will give you the night off."

"It would embarrass your mother, me being here," he added.

"It would do her good," Schuyler replied, a curl to her mouth. "to be taken down a peg or two."

"Well, it won't be by my being here," Boone told her. "Sometimes I think that's a big part of the attraction I have with you---to take your mother down a peg or two. Right?"

"No," she said, rather shocked.

"You sure?"

"Yes. Of course I'm sure."

He looked at her, standing there across the room from her, his hands in his pockets, and, after a minute, he smiled. "All right," he said. "But I don't want to embarrass your mother. I don't want her to have to explain me to all her friends. Not to mention the Governor."

"Oh, yes, I know the Governor would be truly interested in the explanation, too," she replied, and came across the plush, Oriental rug to him. "For your information," she added, reaching up and smoothing down his collar about his tie. "the thing that first attracted me to you was the eyes."

"Is that a fact," he said, putting his arms about her.

"Yes," she told him. "I just couldn't get over those dark eyes of yours."

She was really good to kiss, she had a really nice mouth and Boone thought that, given his druthers, he would rather stand there with her arms about his neck, her fingers in his hair and kiss her all night than do just about anything else he could think of with anybody else. He would rather kiss her anywhere than anything else, it didn't matter that it was in this opulent room with the whisper of the fire warming the air. If he was doing this out in the freezing cold, he'd still be warm, he knew.

Even when Seth cleared his throat delicately from the doorway, they still had a hard time stopping. Boone released her and she smoothed her dress and they faced her brother, who said, with a laugh in his voice: "Sorry to interrupt, but Pa says he wants the both of you to come play billiards. Says you play too, Sis. Mother's gone upstairs; she won't know."

Boone looked at her. "You play?"

"Sometimes," she admitted. "Mother doesn't like it, but I do."

"She's got a good eye," Seth said. "Come on."

Boone offered his arm with a grin, Schuyler took it and when they got to the doorway, she took Seth's on the other side as they walked down the wide hall.

An hour later, Boone rocked home on Roanoke, stabled him in Long Barn, and made the trek up to Old House still feeling comfortably warm and contented. Inside the kitchen, only Tommycat greeted him until he saw the light from the downstairs bedroom that had been his parents'. Hanging his coat and hat, he went to the doorway and stopped to look in.

"What the sam hill are you doing?" he asked her.

Brynn straightened up quickly at the sound. "Good grief you scared me," she replied. She pushed a stray hair back, puffing a little. "When did you get home?"

"Just now. What are you doing?" he repeated.

No one had slept in Amy and Morgan's room since their death. The children seldom even opened the door to it or went inside. Now, however, Brynn had evidently been busy for awhile. The mattress on the bed which had been rolled up was now flat, there were sheets and quilt spread, pillows at the head.

The dresser was in a different position than when Amy had sat there to brush her hair, the desk where Morgan had done the books and which had come with the house, was where the dresser had stood before. There were curtains at the window, even. The other curtains had been taken out long ago and burned because of the fever; Boone recognized the new curtains as having been in Brynn's room. There was her hairbrush on the dressing table, and a wide-toothed comb and hand mirror. The lamp that burned on the side table beside the bed had been in Brynn's room, too.

"I'm moving in here," she told him.

Of course, he had figured that out. "Oh, no you're not," he said.

"Oh, yes, I am," she replied, and went on sweeping under the bed, reaching far under with the broom.

"Oh no, you're not."

"Oh yes, I am."

"Who says?"

"I do."

"Oh? And who died and made you boss?"

She straightened again and looked at him. "Mama and Daddy did," she replied. "And nobody else wanted to step up."

He hesitated. He knew that look in her eye. "The children will have a fit, you moving in here."

"The children already have," she told him. "While you were out doing---whatever you were doing. I figure that, if you want, you can have my room, then that'll just leave Rue and Sorrel sharing a room, and Sorrel won't sleep by herself, anyway. Until Rue goes off to school, then she'll have to. But that won't be till next fall, so we got awhile to get her convinced that she can."

"School?" he echoed, untying his tie and unbuttoning his collar button. "What makes you think that Rue's still going away to school? We never settled that."

"Because she is," Brynn said, still with that stubborn gleam. "Because that's what Mama and Daddy wanted. So she will."

He stayed a moment longer, then headed for the stairs.

"Boone?" she said and turning, he saw her standing in the doorway.

"What?"

"What'd you have to eat? Over there at the Carson's?"

He knew they'd ask. He didn't want to say, but he knew they'd ask. "Roast beef."

"Really?"

"Yes."

"What else?"

"Roasted potatoes," he said reluctantly. "And squash."

"And?"

"And green beans," he said. "In the pot liquor. And rolls with butter. And fruit to start and gravy and layer cake. Chocolate."

She was silent, looking at him, then she swallowed and said: "My goodness."

"Yes," he agreed and started up the stairs.

"Boone?"

"What now?"

"If the children ask, don't tell them what you had to eat. All right?"

He looked down at her from the stairs. "All right," he replied.

-7-

It took Brynn awhile, but she managed to go to the little school in Dooley and speak with the children's teacher, Mrs. Braswell, about the school that her parents had been told about before they died.

Mrs. Braswell was cordial and concerned and said that, yes, she was sure that the school would still be interested in having Jerusha attend. The school had already sent all the applications for scholarships and had actually written asking about the status of her applying, and had been regretful to hear of Jerusha's family situation. They were truly interested in having Jerusha attend, Mrs. Braswell said. Of course, any school would be interested considering the scores on the tests that Jerusha had taken the spring before, and the essays she had written.

"Your sister is truly remarkable," she told Brynn. "Genius level beyond doubt. She could probably take college ranked classes when she starts next fall, but of course, we can't offer them here. Truly remarkable."

"Remarkable," Brynn repeated to Boone later that evening as they sat at the kitchen table looking over the papers. "Well, that's one way to describe her." They both looked over at where the two younger girls were making an excuse for washing dishes. Jerusha had just eaten a mouthful of bubbles and was frothing them back out all over herself.

"Look!" she gargled at Sorrel. "I'm a mad dog! I got hydrophobie! You better run!"

"Thy lord," Brynn said with a sigh as Sorrel shrieked and flung water at her.

"You two settle down," Boone said to them loudly, then added to Brynn: "Good grief, I sound like Daddy. You really think we'll have the money to do this by fall?"

"Yes," Brynn said firmly. "Either that or I'm going to strangle her and do us all a favor. What's the matter, Jimbo?" she added to the boy sitting silent with them. "You're awful down in the mouth. You sick?"

"No," he replied. "Just----does she have to go, Sister?"

Brynn and Boone exchanged looks. Jordan hadn't had much to say for himself all evening, she realized. Jerusha had been all smiles about going away to school and had dominated the conversation, which wasn't uncommon, but Jordan's normal serenity had been different.

"Does she have to go? Well, I guess she doesn't **have** to. But, Mama and Daddy wanted her to give it a try," Brynn told him. "Her teachers think it would be the best for her. You know she's awful smart. Too smart for the school here."

"She's the smart one," Jordan said. "I guess that makes me the dumb one."

"Don't be silly," she told him. "Nobody's as smart as she is. Except when it comes to common sense. She sure don't have much of that. Will you two stop it!" she raised her voice to say to the battle still going on at the sink. "Rue, you're going to be mopping this floor before you're done. And don't get the cat wet, either."

"You don't want her to go, Jordan?" Boone asked him.

The boy sat silent a moment, then saying: "Oh, I don't know. It don't matter." He hefted himself off the chair and went out into the front room. The other two looked at each other.

"It's what Mama and Daddy wanted," Brynn said to her brother.

"You don't have to convince me," Boone replied.

"He's bound to miss her," she added. "They're twins. He'll just have to cope with it, that's all. Like we all have to cope with all of this. None of it is a lot of fun. 'Cept for Rue, that is."

Boone didn't answer. He looked down at the papers again, then toward the front room. "Sometimes, I just think that he don't cope as good as the rest of us," he said thoughtfully. "I just wish she didn't have to go this fall. Maybe the year after."

"Lord, I'll go crazy by that time," Brynn said. "Anyway, you know what Miz Braswell said. That this is an 'opportune time' for her to go. They have the space available, she's at the right age, all that. They say this would be the right year."

"The way it sounds," Boone said, propping his head on his hand. "they'd be happy to have her anytime. Why not give it another year."

"Because this fall is it," Brynn slapped the papers together in a final sort of way. "Ready or not. But mostly," she said. "because I'm afraid if we put it off, something else will come along and then something else and we'll never do it. We can't afford it now, but if we wait, we'll never afford it. Anyway, it's not like she's walking out the door tomorrow. We've got---and Jordan's got---seven months till she has to leave. He'll be better by then. He's just gloomy tonight."

Boone didn't answer. Brynn knew he didn't like it, she knew Jordan didn't like it, but she didn't care. Jerusha was going, if she had to walk her to Virginia herself.

That evening before she went to bed, Brynn sat at her father's desk and began a new series of figures in the big ledger that Morgan had always used for the Old House accounts. She found a new page, put the date and began, feeling as if she had turned over a new leaf indeed. She sat late that night over it, her fingers cramping with cold, until the numbers began to blur together. When she saw the hour, she was appalled. Crazy to be burning money in lamp oil and depriving herself of sleep just to try to figure out where the money was coming from to get them through the rest of the winter.

But, when the next day, she was able to set out some sort of plan for Boone to see, she was gratified at his approval. She had worked out some sort of viable solution to paying Kevin back, setting money aside for next fall's taxes and still able to build up a sizable sum toward clothes, books and train fare for Jerusha's schooling.

"It'll be close," she admitted to her brother as he read down the numbers. "But, as long as we don't have any unexpected expenses, we can do it. And, even if we do, we should have enough time to build it back up between now and then. As long as nothing too drastic happens."

"We need firewood," Boone pointed out.

"You and Jordan will just have to take a Saturday and get to those falls down by the river," she told him. "We're not going to go paying for split wood when we've got all that lying down there. A vegetable garden this year will go a long way toward groceries come summer; maybe I can get some seeds from Kate. She always puts some back."

"All right," Boone said, swinging the ledger closed. "But if we're working all one Saturday on firewood, we're skipping church to make up for it. And that's final."

At least they had eggs and milk, Brynn decided as she milked the cow that evening. And butter thanks to Katie. If that silly red hen would ever go broody and raise some chicks, they could have pullets for meat in a few months. But, in the middle of the winter, they were lucky they were getting any eggs at all.

February dragged its feet, but at last it ended and March began. Brynn wished for spring as she rode Angelina to and from work at Mrs. Darcy's, but, as March sometimes was, it seemed determined to draw winter out in the most perverse of ways. Low, drizzly skies loomed over the hills, soaking them in fog, pushing down into the valleys in cold waves that brought nothing so interesting as snow. The most that happened was icy rain peppered with sleet that invariably blew in of a morning, soaking the children as they walked to school and stinging Brynn's face as she rode to work.

Boone began to get a perpetual worry frown between his black brows at the thought of them fighting their way to and from town while he was assigned inside jobs at the barns over across the river.

He debated on whether to ask Sam if he could ride over to the school to give the girls a lift home on Roanoke, but decided it wasn't worth what he would lose in pay. They couldn't all three ride and that would leave him leading the horse anyway, getting them all just as wet as if they had walked. He was relieved when Clay let it slip that Kevin had been sending Buck in the wagon to ride them all as far as the turn-off up to Old House.

"Don't tell Brynnie," Clay had added in some alarm. "I wasn't supposed to tell; Pa says that she probably won't like it. He says that what she don't know, won't hurt her."

After that, Boone just worried about Brynn herself. You're getting to be an old mother duck, he told himself sternly. Let them alone, for Pete's sake.

He comforted himself with the thought of Sorrel and Jerusha and Jordan in Kevin's wagon, wrapped in the warm quilts that he knew Janine would send. Sorrel was too thin for a girl her age; she didn't need to be walking in the cold. He decided that if Brynn did find out and kick up a stink, he'd put his foot down about it. He wasn't their father, but he sure felt like it.

Brynn paid Kevin the first installment on the loan of the hundred dollars. She knew it was a pittance, and at that rate, she would be paying him the rest of her natural life, but it was the best she could do. Of course Kevin tried to refuse the thin envelope she handed him, but he didn't try too hard. He knew it was hopeless. So, he let her keep her dignity, thanked her for it, then, when she had left and he had opened it, he sighed and shook his head.

At the end of the month, the weather began to settle. The wind blew with the tiniest bit of a caress to it, rather than an edge, there was a scent blowing from the woods of thawing earth. It was still bitterly cold in the mornings, but the rains stopped and the sky that domed above the pastureland was robin's egg blue. By the time the children were coming home, they were carrying their coats and hats.

Kevin was in town one sunny Tuesday morning and thinking to himself that it would be time to move the herd from the bottomland soon. The bottomland near the Soque had the best grazing in the winter months, but it also was first to flood in the spring when rain tended to come unexpectedly.

After the first couple of years in Dooley, he and Morgan had learned to move the herd early in the spring to the higher ground, although that sometimes meant feeding them hay while the bottomland grass was temptingly green. After a few sudden thunderstorms rolling down from the hills and a day or two in the pouring rain gathering the herd out of harm's way from flood waters, they had learned that it saved a lot of headaches.

He had just gotten the mail from the post office and was leafing through the few letters when someone spoke to him and turning, he saw Adam crossing the street to meet him. Kevin greeted him with a genuine smile that made the similarities between him and his son very evident. He had tried to not look up his second eldest every time he went to town, although he was sorely tempted to, for Kevin worried about him more than he let on. Although he had known as long as everybody else that the boy's marriage was not good, he didn't like to see it dissolve. There had never been a divorce in the family as far as anybody knew; he didn't know what to make of one now.

"You taking the day off?" Adam asked cheerily enough after they had said their hellos.

"Picking up fence," Kevin nodded to the wagon pulled up nearby. "That big snow pulled down a section near Elisha's grave. Need to get it fixed before we move the herd."

"Need any help when you do move it?" the other asked.

His father looked at him. "You volunteering?"

"For a home cooked meal from Ma I am," he grinned.

"Well, good grief, you don't need to herd cattle to come eat with us, you know."

"I know," the smile faded a bit. "But I don't want to be coming around every other minute crying on your shoulder and eating your food, either."

"You're hardly doing that," Kevin told him. "We'll probably move the herd end of the week. Come out on Friday morning and help and stay for supper. Your mother will be pleased to have you. She misses you."

"All right," he said after a pause. "I'll take the day off from the tanner's. My boss won't mind. Business is a little slow."

"You seen the bunch up at Old House?" Kevin asked next. They both moved aside so they could talk out of the way.

Adam looked at him quickly, but his father's face only showed friendly concern. "Not recently," he replied slowly. "I figured I wouldn't be much welcome up there. Not by Boone, anyway."

"There's more up there than Boone."

"Yes," he agreed. "And that's who Boone wants me to stay away from."

"Can't blame him, can you?" Kevin observed mildly.

"No, Pa I can't blame him," Adam replied, a bit testily. "That's what I mean. I can't blame him but he can't blame me, either. I just feel like I feel about her." He paused and then asked: "How are they doing, anyway? I heard about her and that Darcy fellow wrecking that sleigh. Is she all right? She didn't look too good that day down when she was at New House...."he stopped.

Kevin looked at him. "You saw Brynn that day, did you?"

"Well," Adam said. "I ran into her coming out of the house as I was going in, that's all."

"I see," his father said. "And she's fine. They seem to be doing all right all in all."

"That's good," he said, pushing his hands into his coat pockets. His restless black eyes looked out over the usual midday bustle of Dooley business district.

His father watched him in the brief pause. He had always been the most handsome of his sons, taller than Buck with a lift to his chin that made him look taller yet, his dark glossy hair catching the sun, the glint in his eye that could change from anger to laughter in a heartbeat. Of all three of the brothers, he had always been the one with the most going for him; it puzzled Kevin how his life tended to keep straying from one dissatisfaction to another.

"Heard from Bethy?" he asked him abruptly.

Adam gave a short laugh. "Yes, she wrote," he said. "To tell me they are both fine, that Gid says hello, all the usual nice nothing that strangers write to each other."

"Did she say anything about---well---anything else?"

"What could she say? That she misses me? That she wants to come back? She won't say any of that."

"I'm sorry to hear that," his father said.

"Well, I'm not surprised," the other replied. "There isn't really a lot to be said that hasn't been said a hundred times. I just hate that Gid's caught in the middle, that's all."

"You planning on going to Duggansville to see him?"

"What, you mean ever? Yes, of course I am. Don't know when, exactly." His eyes sought the street before them again, not meeting his father's gaze. "I'm too mad right now to trust myself being in the same room with her. That wouldn't do Gideon any good, either, would it?"

"No, I suppose not," Kevin allowed. "You need to work toward it, though. Even if you still have hard feelings toward his mother, you can't stay away from him too long. Surely the two of you can be civil to each other for his sake while he's within earshot."

"Yes, that's true, I suppose," Adam replied. "I wish he was a bit older. I'd have him with me in a heartbeat if he was. I swear I would, Bethy or no Bethy."

Kevin was about to reply when someone called to him and turning, he saw a tall, thin figure coming toward them down the sidewalk from uptown. After a moment, he recognized it to be Nimrod Webb from the bank. It was so seldom that he saw Webb out of his office, he did a double take at the lanky, long-legged figure, his coat flapping open in the chilly wind as he strode quickly toward them.

The man had a craggy, deeply-creased face, thinning hair and the pasty complexion of a man who rarely came outside in the weather, but he wasn't a bad sort and had been very helpful after Morgan and Amy's deaths. Kevin greeted him warmly.

"You won't be so happy to see me, I'm afraid, after you hear why I ran you down," Webb replied, puffing a little. "I was going to ride out your way to talk to you if I hadn't chanced to see you just now."

"What is it?" Kevin asked him.

"Well," the man looked at Adam then back at Kevin, his face reddening a little. "I hate to talk about such things out on a public street, but I thought you'd want to know. That note on your brother's loan is come due and, as yet, we haven't received any payment on it. Not one. As you know, I went over it all with you nephew and you back before the new year, right after your brother's unfortunate passing, and it was due----the first payment---at the end of January. Since then, the next month and the next have gone by and...."

"Oh, Lord," Kevin groaned. "They haven't paid any?"

"No, sir, I'm sorry to say they haven't."

"How much do they owe?" Adam asked.

Mr. Webb looked uncomfortable and Kevin told him: "Too much. Anything is too much. I'm sorry, Webb," he said. "I'm sure it's an oversight on their part. I'll---I'll talk to Boone about it and get back with you."

"Mr. McKenna, I need to let you know," Webb told him. "That we need the last two payments, at least, by the end of the month or---well---it's the bank policy to foreclose on the property."

"Foreclose?" Adam echoed.

"Yes, I know," Kevin told the banker. "I'll let Boone know."

When Webb had gone and they were alone, Adam said to his father: "Is he talking about foreclosing on Old House?"

Kevin pushed his hat back and sighed. Ten minutes ago he was thinking about nothing more serious than when to get to the fence at the river, then his son had come with his delightful observations on the state of his marriage and now this. "That's standard procedure," he said. "But it's not going to happen."

"How are you going to stop it?"

Kevin's mouth was set in a way that was very familiar to his son. "I don't know," he told him. "But it's not going to happen."

Sam Carson was sitting his big bay cutting horse up by the fence when Kevin rode up onto the Big House property. It was a chilly, early spring day, the kind that felt hardly warmer than winter, when the breeze had a wet slap to it that belied the budding trees and new grass. Kevin rode to the big man and Sam greeted him with a smile.

He had always been on good terms with all the McKennas on the other side of the river; he had found them to be the sort he could relate to---hard-working, mind-your-own-business type of men who looked you in the eye and didn't stand on ceremony. Sam found the pretentiousness of his wife's more affluent friends to be just a bit grating on his sensibilities.

He and Kevin sat on their horses and talked about the state of the new calves born this year, on whether the snow of the past winter would be enough to raise the water table from the dry couple of years they had had, and when plowing should be started. Then, Kevin nodded toward where some of the hired men were working and asked if he could borrow one of them for a minute.

Sam looked toward them and replied: "I suppose you mean your nephew, Boone, do you?"

"Yes, if I could," Kevin said. "I just need to speak to him for a minute or two. You can have him right back."

"I think that could be arranged," Sam told him and, whistling between his teeth, called out: "McKenna!" and gestured.

As Boone made his trudging way up the slope toward them, Kevin asked: "How's the boy working out, then?"

"Oh, he'll do," Sam replied with a smile. "He's one of the few I don't send on his way when the work goes slack. Course, if I did that, my daughter would have my head, so I wouldn't dare, anyway." Then, as the young man came up to them: "Boone, your uncle needs a word with you. Take a break and then get right back at it." With a nod to Kevin, he moved his horse up the track toward the barns.

Kevin dismounted and he and Boone walked a short distance from the fence, then, turning his back on the group down the hill in the pasture, Kevin said quietly: "Boone, I had a little talk with Nimrod Webb in town this morning."

Boone took off his hat and pushed his sweaty hair back with one forearm before replacing it. In spite of the chill, the work had warmed him up. "You did?" he said.

Kevin gave him a keen look, but the boy met his gaze directly, his dark eyes clear. "Yes, he ran me down to talk to me, actually," he went on. "He was concerned about that note that Old House owes. He says that there's been no payment made since the first of the year."

Boone looked puzzled. "Note?" he said. "What note? On Old House?"

"Yes, don't you remember? We talked about it last fall right after your folks---well, when you and I went down to the bank and met with Webb about your Daddy's accounts. Your Daddy took out a loan with Old House as collateral for that new well he had to sink a couple of years ago, after he got back on his feet after the accident." Suddenly, he saw realization begin in the boy's face. Boone took a quick intake of breath. "There've been payments due on it since then, which I know Morgan was making, and then I paid up with the part of the herd I sold off from Old House. That brought it current up to the end of last year, but when you bunch took over Old House...."

"Ohhh," Boone said and Kevin's heart sank. "Oh shit."

"You remember?"

"I do now," Boone said. "Oh, my God." He put a hand to his head. "Oh my God, Kev, I forgot all about it."

"You forgot?"

"Yes. Oh God, Kevin, I forgot about it. We were supposed to be paying on it, too, weren't we?"

"Does Brynnie know about it? Did you ever tell her...?"

"No. I clean---I just forgot about it. How could I have forgotten about it?"

"Well, you have had a lot on your mind lately."

The boy threw his arms up in the air, slapped his hat on his leg, raising a cloud of dust. "How could I have been so

stupid!" A few heads turned from down the hill. "What did he say, anyway?" he asked more quietly.

Kevin sighed. "There wasn't much he could say. He says he needs two payments before the end of the month."

Boone stared. "The end of **this** month?"

"Yes."

"**Two** payments?"

"Yes."

"Two payments, two months' worth by the end of the month."

"So he says."

"Or what?"

"Or---," he hesitated, but he had to tell him. "Or he says they'll have to foreclose on Old House."

The boy's face turned pale under its layer of dust. "Oh, no."

"So he says," his uncle said again.

"Oh, no," Boone repeated.

"Boone," Kevin said. "We won't let it happen. I don't---I don't know really what we'll do, but we won't let that happen, all right? There's the auction coming up in a couple of weeks, maybe...."

"No, Kev, that's all right," he told him and, despite his ashy color, his voice was firmer. "You can't keep bailing us out all the time. We're already indebted to you."

"Boone, it's family..."

"I know it's family," he said, a bit abruptly. "and this end of the family will figure out something, that's all. Thanks just the same. We got into this, we'll....we'll figure something out." His eyes wandered away at nothing, he ran a hand through his sweaty hair again. "Brynnie's going to kill me."

Kevin said nothing. He didn't envy him telling her, that was for sure.

"You did what!" she said, her eyes wide.

"I just---forgot," Boone said again. "But, look that's not the point, now. We've got to figure out a way…"

"You just forgot?" Brynn said incredulously, staring at him. They were standing in Old House kitchen, supper was over, dishes were done, and he had waited as long as he could before he told her. The others were in the front room, it was Friday night, and there was a checker game going on. Jerusha loved checkers. "You just forgot that we owe a note on Old House? And it's how much?"

He told her and she threw her hands up in the air, very much the way he had done a few hours before. "How much a month?"

"Hundred and fifty."

"Hundred and fifty **dollars**! And they want two months worth in three weeks?"

"Yes," he said miserably. "I'm sorry, Brynn."

"Sorry? Yes, I do think I quite agree with you. So, we have to come up with three hundred dollars in three weeks, then an extra hundred and fifty dollars a month after that. Oh, my God." She went to the window seat and sat down with energy, one foot tucked under her. "Well," she said after a moment. "Looks like you and Uncle Kevin and Janny and all of you will get what you want after all. Old House is gone. There is no way in hell we can pay that. They'll just foreclose on Old House, the children will be split up, we'll be just everybody's poor relations, and you can go on your merry way being responsible for nobody. What a nice way to settle everything. Congratulations."

"Now wait a minute," he said. "Don't go implying that I did this on purpose…."

"Oh, of course not. Just very convenient, that's all, isn't it?"

"I may be stupid, but I didn't go planning all this."

"You never wanted to do Old House, anyway," she fired at him. "You were happy the way things were. I had to practically twist your arm off to get you to even try it."

"That's not true and you know it."

"Do I? I don't think I do. I think your little lapse in memory is making you very, very happy right about now. You don't care about Old House. You don't care about the children being lumped in with Kevin and Janny's children. You don't care about Jerusha going away to school; you never wanted her to go in the first place. Now, she won't be. Isn't that a relief?"

"I'm not going away to school?" came the voice from the doorway, and Boone saw the children there, watching. "I thought..."Jerusha said.

"I have pulled my weight every bit as much as anybody else in this damn family," Boone said, getting angry in his turn. "And you can't say different. You were the one who went off joy-riding with Steve Darcy in a stolen sleigh and nearly got killed and cost us a hundred dollars."

"Which I am paying off!" Brynn was back on her feet now, they faced each other. "I am paying it off by working for that old witch I work for but all you want to do is go over to Carson's and eat fancy dinners and screw Carson's daughter!"

"You shut up about that!"

"I will not!"

"You shut up! You've been a boil on the butt of this family ever since you decided to start Old House," he shouted at her. "You bitch and moan and boss these children around----won't let us light a lamp or burn a stove till Sorrel's sick with the cold, feed them next to nothing---look at Jordan! He's thin as a rail, their clothes are in tatters, the house is filthy."

"You could help too, you know!"

"I do help! We all help, but it's not good enough for you. Maybe Kevin and Janny should take these children back. Maybe---maybe the best thing that could happen would be to lose Old House."

He stopped and they looked at each other, both breathing quickly. He was so angry, he could've slapped her. Over at the doorway, Sorrel was crying quietly.

"Oh, to hell with all of you then," Brynn said, grabbed her coat off the rack and left.

There was a pause when the only sound was Sorrel sniffling. After a moment, Boone went to the little group, pulled her to him and patted her back roughly.

"It's all right, Shrimp," he said. "It'll all be all right."

"Will I get to go to school?" Jerusha asked in a thin voice.

"Yes," he said firmly. "Yes, you will."

Brynn rode Angelina at as fast a run as she could dare on the wet road until the dashing wind made her breathless. She rode her until she was nearing town and she had stopped crying and she had her anger under control. Then, she drew rein and slowed her to a canter, then a trot, and tried to think. Her hair was straggling down; she pushed it back hopelessly. She had come out without her hat or gloves and she was beginning to shiver.

"I won't go back," she said half-aloud. "Not yet, anyway." But she was cold and getting closer and closer to town and then there would probably be somebody on the road she would know and they would recognize her and then they would want to know what she was doing out there in the dark and would ask if she was all right. And she wasn't. But she didn't want anybody else to know.

She hated Boone with all of her might, but it didn't solve anything. She didn't even know if she wanted to solve anything. She didn't know what she wanted. She didn't know if she wanted Old House or keeping the children together or any of it.

If she didn't have Old House and the children, she could quit work at Old Darcy's and live with Kate and have a life of her own. Maybe she could go back to school---no, she didn't want that. But, she could have a life.

She could help Katie with Brett and Amelia and just live for awhile. Jerusha could go to school because Kevin and Janine would find the money to send her, and Jordan could work just when he wanted to and eat Janine's cooking and Sorrel could be warm all the time. And Boone could go on off with Schuyler Carson and not have all the rest of them to worry about. All nice and tidy. Maybe that would be better.

Then she thought about her Mama and Daddy. She thought about Mama laughing at something Jordan had done, or her Daddy watching them from over out of the way in the shadows on the porch, or how Sorrel would curl up on his lap in the evening.

And how Old House looked from down at Long Barn when it was dark and the windows would be lighted with gold, and how the Coming Home bell would ding just a little when the breeze would catch it, and how the sweep of land would open up down from the bay window in the kitchen.

She was crying again then. She gulped tears and her cheeks were cold with them and when she kicked Angelina back into a canter, they whipped sideways out of her eyes. Suddenly, she knew where she wanted to go and who she wanted to see. She pulled Angelina abruptly, so abruptly that she gave a little rear before turning down the side street just this side of the business end of town. She knew, at least, where she wanted to go. She had made that decision, anyway. And, before she got there, she managed to make herself stop crying.

The nice soft blurred feeling was getting on toward the blank dead feeling, and Adam knew that he'd probably wake up on the settee again because he wouldn't be able to make it to the bed, but that was all right by him. He didn't much like sleeping in his clothes, but taking them off and walking all across the house to the bedroom and getting undressed was way too much trouble.

It didn't matter to anybody, anyway, whether he slept on the settee or in a bed like a civilized person, or if he undressed or slept in his clothes. Just as long as he was cleaned up and wide awake for work in the morning, that was all anybody cared. And he always was. At least he could say that he had always been up and ready for anything by the morning.

When Bethy was around, he never would have dared do any of this, of course, he thought swilling the whiskey around in the bottle. He was getting near the bottom, he could finish it up before the dark took him over again.

Bethy would have never stood for any of this, he knew. She would have been shocked at the state he now found himself. She would have stopped in her tracks at the state of the little house she had left. That thought made him smile a little. He rather liked the idea of shocking her by the mess her house was now.

When the knock came at the door, he almost thought he had imagined it.

He was bordering on sleep, or a drunken stupor or something, and the wind had sent a branch tapping at the window incessantly, so he almost disregarded it. Then it came again, a soft knock it was true, tentative really, but definitely a knock on the little front door that opened out onto the tiny front porch. Adam groaned. The absolutely last thing he needed right then was a visitor; God forbid that it be one of his parents. He almost didn't answer it. There wasn't a person in the world that he really wanted to see. Well, that was almost true...

When he heaved himself up and made his way to the door and opened it, he had to close his eyes a time or two and open them again to be really sure he was seeing who he thought he was seeing. He leaned one arm on the door jam and stared.

"Brynn," he said.

She was staring at him, too. "Hello," she replied.

"What are you doing here?" he asked.

"I---," she said, stopped, and then said: "I needed to see you. Can I?"

"Can you---? Oh, can you come in, you mean? Sure," he stepped aside and let her step into the front room. "Sorry," he added, closing the door. "At the mess, I mean."

She was standing quite still and staring at it all, just like he had been staring at her. She was staring at the buck stove with the door open because of the spilling ashes among the fading coals, at the bed-pillow on the rumpled settee with the blanket stained and smelly, at the dirty dishes on the table, at the bottles around. He couldn't blame her really. And he couldn't take his eyes off her.

At last, she looked at him again and, to his surprise, he saw around the remains of tears, that she was angry.

"And Boone says Old House is bad," she said.

He pushed his hair back and shrugged. "I said it was a mess," he told her.

"Well, you were right about that."

He went, with some difficulty, to the table and sat down heavily. "I'm right about something, anyway."

She came further into the room, picked up a dropped shirt and moved it to the settee. "It didn't used to be like this here," she said.

"No, well, a lot of things are different now," he propped up his head on his hand.

"Since Bethy left, you mean."

"Since Bethy left," he agreed. "I guess it's been about a year since you were here, hasn't it? A lot has happened in this past year. Who'd have thought then that we'd be where we are now."

She didn't reply. She was still drifting about the room.

"I miss your parents," he told her. She looked at him quickly. "I loved your mama to pieces. She was great. She'd give me hell from time to time, but that was a good thing, I guess. She raised me as much as my own ma did. I told Bethy that once. She didn't understand..." his voice trailed away. After a moment, he added: "Bethy didn't understand a lot of things."

"Do you think Bethy would understand this place?"Brynn asked sharply.

"What place?"

"This," she said, picking up another piece of clothing from the piles around. "This pig-sty you've got here. What would she think of this? Adam, have you been living like this since she left?"

"Pretty much."

"This is a disgrace," she said to him. Her dark brows which he had always fancied tracing with his fingers were drawn down in such a frown, he was surprised at her. "It stinks of bad food and dirty clothes and I bet you don't have a clean dish in the place. Is this how you're going to live now?"

"I haven't decided," he told her. "What do you suggest?"

"I suggest you take a good look at yourself," she said. "and think about what kind of a father you want to be to your little boy. You've still got one, you know."

"Yes, I realize that."

"Do you? You think any father worth having would sit around in this state? Your father wouldn't."

"Oh, of course not. Not Kevin McKenna."

"No, not Kevin McKenna. Nor Morgan, either. What would your mother think of this, Adam? Forget about Bethy; what about your mother? Surely she hasn't been over and seen this."

"No, she hasn't been over here and seen this," he replied. "And for your information, I'm free, white, and twenty-one and I can live like I want to, thank you."

"And this is how you want to live?" she asked.

He rubbed his face. He had his usual five-o'clock shadow and it rasped against his palm. "I don't know what I want," he said.

Brynn sighed. "Go wash, for Pete's sake," she told him. She was taking off her coat and rolling up her sleeves. He sat and watched her. "Go on," she repeated, bundling up her hair. He realized now that it was hanging loose down her back. She tied it back and then, when he still didn't move, she went to him, pulling him to his feet. "If you can walk," she added in derision. "Go wash and change your clothes. I can at least get them in to soak." She shoved him toward the bedroom.

"Can I have some hot water?" he asked.

"Yes, go on. I'll see if the kettle's hot. Is it? Did you put it on?"

"I don't know."

She brought it to him as he was finding the wash basin on its stand under more dirty clothes. He had stripped off his shirt and was groggily gratified that she noticed when she handed him the kettle. She averted her eyes, told him to not burn himself and left.

He heard her clanking dishes around in the kitchen while he was washing. He decided to go whole hog and shave, finding it not as difficult as he had thought it would be in his condition. Somehow, having Brynn here and then scrubbing with soap and water had sobered him up a bit.

Brynn had, for her part, decided that a good swig or two might not be amiss and had helped herself to the remnants at the bottom of the bottle she found on the counter. It was horribly strong and burned and left her breathless, but she took another swallow before she started pumping water into the sink. Men, she thought to herself. Damn men. She wished wholeheartedly that she could be like them.

She picked up every piece of dirty laundry she could find, filled the boiler with water, put it on the stove and pushed the fire into a flaming furnace to heat it. Poking in clothes and soap flakes, she left it and discovering an empty box, began disposing of old bottles, relishing the clank and rattle. She hoped Adam would come out and ask what all the racket was about; she had a few more words of wisdom for him.

She was finishing sweeping up the spilled ashes from the buck stove hearth when there was a step behind her and, turning with brush and dust pan in hand, she saw that he was improved somewhat. She wiped the back of one hand over her forehead as Adam looked about the room appraisingly.

"Looks a lot better," he admitted. "Do we have to have the windows open?"

"For me to be able to breathe, yes," she replied, dumping ashes into the scuttle. "You'll need to empty this in the morning."

"I will. Thanks," he said. "Is there---um---coffee?"

"Coffee? Yes, there's coffee if you want some."

"I thought I smelled some. Anyway, that was the idea, yes. Get me clean and sober. Presentable, even." He straightened his cuffs and ran both hands through his damp hair.

"That wasn't the idea I had when I came over here," Brynn said dryly, brushing her hands off, replacing the fireplace tools and heading back for the kitchen. "I didn't come over to do your housework and place nursemaid to you."

He followed, watching her move about his house as if it was her own. She got down a cup, poured it full from the perking pot on the stove, and shoved it at him unceremoniously, standing back with her arms folded.

"It's probably not very good," she told him. "Boone says my coffee stinks. And I'm not going to wash your clothes. They can soak overnight, then you're on your own with that. Maybe your mama will come over and do it."

"So why, then?" he asked, blowing steam away and sipping tentatively.

"Why what?"

"Why did you come over?"

She was silent. She looked at him, at the man that she had known most of her life from the boy he used to be, and thought about all the different ways she could answer that question, then decided to just say it.

"I needed to see you," she replied.

"Why?"

Instantly, she felt the tears spring back to her eyes. "They---they're going to foreclose on Old House," she said and heard them in her voice, too.

"I know," he told her.

"You know?" she echoed. "How do you know?"

"I was with Pa in town when Webb talked to him."

She leaned back against the sink with a bump. "So, does everybody know about it? Am I the last one in town to hear?"

"I have no idea. Probably not."

"I bet your mother knows, though."

"I bet she does too. Pa tells her everything." He drank some more, watching her as she wiped her eyes hurriedly. "How much do you owe?" he asked at length.

"Six hundred dollars. We have to pay three hundred of it by the end of the month."

"I don't have it," he said. "I wish I did."

"I know you don't have it," she told him. "That's why I came over, because I know you don't have it."

"So why did you come over to tell me, then?"

She was hugging herself as if she was cold. "Because that's what I always do," she said. "Always come running after you. I always have."

She looked so young and lost and cold, standing there with her hair beginning to tumble down again. She looked so young and lost and cold, he set his cup aside and went to her and enfolded her in his arms. He pushed her head against his chest, feeling her put her arms about his waist and her hair fall heavy over his hands out of its hurried bundle.

"I've always come running after you," she repeated against him. "I can't stop running after you. Why can't I stop running after you?"

"Because I can't stop running after you, either," he said and tipped her face up to him.

He kissed her long and slow and tasted her mouth, and could tell that she had been kissed like that before. She knew what he was doing. For a long moment, she responded to him, then she pulled back, but not out of his arms, and said breathlessly:

"Adam, no. We can't...."

"Yes, we can," he told her. "And who's been kissing you like this?"

"That's none of your business," she told him, still breathing hard.

"That's true," he admitted. "But right now, it's just you and me, Little One." He used his smile with the name he used to call her. She had always loved his smile. He looked right into those deep, gold-flecked eyes. "Who's to stop us? Who's to care? You've been doing everything on your own, Brynn. Everything. Do something for you, just this once. Just one time. Like it was always supposed to be."

He knew she would. There had been very few women Adam couldn't have when he set his mind to it and he knew he could have had her years before. He knew she would let him now.

And she did. She tried, some time later in her life, to think that maybe it was because she'd had two swallows of whiskey, or that she was tired with everything, or she was mad at Kevin and Janny and it was a way to get back at them, or it was a way to get back at her parents. But, even when she had begun to think that, she knew it wasn't true. She just plain didn't care any more and the act of letting Adam take her clothes from her there in the house he had shared with his wife was very sweet.

She gave in to him effortlessly, let him lift the locket chain over her head, lay her down and put his hands and mouth on her. Her body was full and smooth and silky to the touch for him, as his was lean and hard for her. She told him while she still had breath to speak that: I've never done this before. Adam, I've never done this…And he shushed her down and smiled at her and said that he knew. He told her: Just let it happen, Brynnie. Just let me do it…And then it was so intense, she couldn't have stopped if she had wanted to.

She was every bit as good as he had always imagined she would be. He had imagined her for years, had decided and then had discarded the thought of being where he now found himself. He had given it all up, and now she was here and he wooed her with every skill he had acquired, watching it all be new and astonishingly sensual for her.

Her inhibitions dropped away one by one like the layers of clothes had; she found herself laying herself open for him, he found himself having to be the one who slowed them down. And when at last it was all deep pleasure, she found herself lost in the excruciatingly sweet painfulness that swirled her away into the dark. She let him and let him and did it with him and it was exactly the way he had imagined it would be and better…..

She woke suddenly.

She knew immediately where she was and what she had done. She had been dreaming about it and the dream blended into the reality of it when she woke with her head on his chest and his arms about her. She lay and looked at the yellow flame of the lamp that still burned on the table beside the bed. It burned with a low flame, as if it had burned a long time. It was still dark outside, but there was a dim grayness in the black that said how near the dawn was. She moved her face against him and tasted his skin, then slid out from under his arm and out of the bed to dress soundlessly, watching him sleep. When she had pulled on her shoes and coat, put her locket in her pocket, she bent and blew out the lamp. She was out of the house and cantering toward home on Angelina before the smoke had drifted away.

Boone was sitting at the kitchen table when she had stabled her horse and walked in the back door.

She stopped still a moment, her hand on the doorknob, the door still open with the gray streaks of dawn behind her over the crest of the nearest hills. Then, she came inside, closed the door and took off her coat.

"Where the hellfire and damnation have you been?" Boone asked her in the exasperation of hours worrying. She didn't answer and, when she turned back from the rack and he saw her face, he added: "Oh, no. Don't tell me."

"Tell you what?"

"You've been with him, haven't you?"

"With who?"

"With who. With Adam, of course. You have, haven't you? You don't have to say a word, I can tell."

"I'm not going to talk about this with you. We've got other things to talk about."

Boone stared at her. "That sonofabitch took you to bed, didn't he!"

"I said I'm not going to talk to you about that," she repeated. "I know a way to get the money we owe on the house."

He got to his feet slowly, as if he was years older and tired. "You stay out all night with Adam and you say you don't want to say anything about it? What the hell does that mean?"

"It means it's none of your business, Boone."

"Like hell it isn't!"

"Like hell it isn't, right. Listen to what I said. I know where we can get the money for the house. If you say one more word about anything else but how we are going to get the money for the house, I'm leaving and you won't see me again. Now, listen to me."

He stood with his hands on his hips and faced her. After a long moment, he said: "All right. How?"

Brynn sighed. "We can sell the horses."

"What!"

"We can sell the horses. Not Roanoke. You need him for work. But Angy and Israel, we can sell at the auction."

"Sell Angy? Sell Mama's horse? Are you crazy?"

"I'm not crazy and she's my horse now. There's the auction coming up next weekend. We can put them both up separate, Angy first. Maybe she'll bring enough that we don't have to sell Israel and Jordan can keep him for working. Daddy always had people coming up to him asking what he would take for her. She should bring a good price, you know she should."

"Brynn, you can't sell Angelina," Boone told her, aghast.

"Yes, I can and I will. We can't sell the cattle we got down at New House yet. Most of them are in calf and they'll be worth twice in the fall auction. And we need that money for taxes and for Jerusha's schooling come fall. This way, we'd have the money fast for the mortgage, we'll still have the cattle for taxes. It's the only way."

"You can't sell Angelina."

"Boone, listen to me," she said, taking a step nearer. "It's the only way. Maybe we won't have to sell Israel, but if we do, Jordan can borrow a horse from Kevin for work. But we have to sell Angelina."

He just looked at her. Then, he said: "You sure it's worth it?"

"Yes," she replied instantly. "Of course it is. Yes, it's worth it. Don't you think it's worth it, Boone?"

Before he could answer, the door opened suddenly and Adam was there. It was so sudden and so unexpected, they both jumped. His presence filled the room, as it always had. They hadn't heard him ride up; they hadn't heard anything but themselves. He had been riding hard; his hair was blown around, the dark curliness flipped out from under his hat, and he was out of breath from his run up the hill.

"Brynn," he said. "I have to see you."

Boone put himself between them. "You bastard!" he said. "You've seen quite enough of her."

"Boone," Brynn said, catching his arm. He jerked away.

"What the hell kind of nerve you got coming over here?"

Adam never switched his gaze from her. "I have to talk to you."

"Boone," Brynn came around to face him. "Stop." She stood and looked at him until he met her gaze. "It's all right," she told him. "Let me talk to him."

She saw the inward struggle going on in her brother. After a moment, he stepped around her and saying to Adam: "You need to be off this property in five minutes." He left the room. They heard his boot heels on the stairs, but neither saw him go.

When they were alone, Adam took his hat off and tossed it to the table. "Why did you leave?" he asked her.

"I had to come home," she replied. She took hold of the back of the kitchen chair. She couldn't quite look at him; she couldn't stop looking at him.

"Why did you leave like that?" he amended. "You didn't say good-bye."

She was silent a moment, then told him: "You called me Bethy last night."

She was looking right at him as she said it and she saw his face change. "Oh, God," he said. Then: "God, Brynnie, I'm sorry…"

"Adam," she said. "You need to go to Duggansville and be with your wife. And your son."

"Brynn…"

"You need to go be with your wife," she repeated. Going to the door, she opened it for him and stepped aside, holding the doorknob.

He didn't move. "I don't want to be with her," he said.

"Yes, you do," she replied. "You love her."

He still didn't move. Brynn started to shake down inside herself.

"I want to be with you," he said at last.

"No, you don't," she told him. "All you wanted to do with me was what you did last night. That's all you ever wanted to do with me."

"That's not true."

"Yes, it is."

"You wanted it the same," he said. "and you know it. You can't tell me different."

"Of **course** I wanted it."

"And you loved it as much as I did. It was good---you and me."

"Of course it was good. You know it was."

He shifted toward her and then stopped. "And so…"

"You need to go to Duggansville," she said. "You need to leave this house. Now."

She didn't raise her eyes. The shaking was worse. She was afraid he would see it. She could feel him all through her, she could feel him breathing. After a pause, he picked up his hat and went to the doorway, but there he stopped. She didn't look at his face. She kept her eyes on his hand on the door jam beside her.

"This is not over, Brynn," he said and left.

When Boone came back down, she was sitting at the kitchen table, her face in her hands, trying to stop shaking. He took a quick look around and said:

"He's gone, then."

"He's gone," she replied, raising her head. She got to her feet and sighed. "It's market day. You'll go?"

He was looking at her differently. She didn't like it, but she supposed that she couldn't much blame him. "I'll go," he replied. "Give me an hour's sleep, and me and Shrimp'll go." She nodded and headed for the bedroom at the foot of the stairs, but when he asked: "What if we don't get enough money for the mortgage even selling both horses?" she stopped and replied:

"It'll be enough to keep the bank happy awhile. If---if we don't, then I'll---I'll get a second job. On the weekends. Yes," she said, half to herself. "I can get a second job on the weekends. That'll work." She rubbed the back of her neck up under the long tail of hair tied back. "I'll take Angy and ride into town later this morning and register them for the auction. Mr. Barnes is holding the registration, isn't he?"

"I think so," Boone told her.

He watched her go to the door of the bedroom, then said: "I'll go get them registered when I'm in town. Save you a trip."

She looked back at him in tired surprise. "Thanks."

"Well," he said. "No sense in both of us going to town today. And if," he added, stopping her again. "if anybody's going to get a second job, it'll be me."

-8-

The next Saturday morning, Brynn curried Angelina more carefully than she ever had before.

She brushed her and combed her black mane and tail, seeing how the mane fell unfashionably long like a mustang, and the tail sweeping nearly to the ground. Then, she took a rag and polished her body until she shone, brushing away the remnants of her winter coat. Angelina was one of the kind that shed her coat early, and now it was an advantage.

The blue-gray with the black markings and creamy rump with black splashes was bold and bright and would have made Brynn want to cry if she had let herself. She cleaned the hooves carefully, painted them with oil, then gave a final rub to her tapered face. The large, clear eyes regarded her.

Beside her at the fence outside Long Barn, Jordan was doing the same with Israel. She almost hated having him do that more than she would have if he hadn't done it. Both the little girls had howled for most of the week about selling the two horses, but Jordan hadn't. Now, he helped her groom the old paint pony that Morgan had given to Boone when he was about Jordan's age and on which all the children had learned to ride.

Brynn almost wished Jordan would say something about it all. But Jordan seemed to grasp the situation even more readily than Boone; he curried and brushed and combed Israel and had not a bad word to say.

Then she sent the girls down to hitch a ride with Kevin and Janine to the fairgrounds and she and Jordan and Boone rode the horses down. If all went well, Boone would be the only one riding back. They didn't ride along with Kevin's wagon. The three of them rode some distance behind and none spoke.

The fairgrounds at Dooley was nothing more than a big, open field with a few paddocks that occasionally were widened when the fall cattle auction deemed it necessary. Once in a blue moon, a traveling carnival came through and then the fairgrounds were really fairgrounds. On the Fourth of July, they were used for the greased pig chase and the greased pole climb and the egg-n-spoon race.

In the spring, however, there was a good-sized horse auction, and this year, Brynn saw with a mixture of fear and relief that there was a crowd to rival the one that came to bid on cattle. Sometimes the horse auction didn't attract many buyers. This time, it seemed that it was.

"There's Sam Carson's team he's selling," Boone pointed them out. They were a matched pair of Percherons standing alone in one paddock; huge, gray-dappled and calm.

Sam Carson himself was there, with his foreman and, as they approached, the tall, slender girl with curling dark hair stepped forward to the fence. Boone touched his hat brim to Schuyler and they both smiled.

"You can go on with her if you want to," Brynn told him. He looked at her in surprise. "Me and Jordan can get the horses where they're supposed to be. Go ahead."

"That's all right," Boone replied. "I'll look her up later. I'll give y'all a hand."

He looked back over one shoulder at the girl with her father and then Brynn looked back too. Schuyler blinked. They were as if cast from the same mold.

It was a long day. It seemed as if the time would never come when Angelina would be up. Brynn stood apart from everybody, alternating between chewing her fingernails and stroking the gray mare. Angelina didn't seem to think that anything was out of the ordinary; she watched the other horses with interest but not alarm, allowed any number of people to handle her, and was always glad when one of the family came and talked to her. Jerusha and Sorrel made nuisances of themselves, looking woebegone and teary-eyed when anyone came near the two horses until Brynn told them to go somewhere else or die.

"You wouldn't be saying that if Uncle Kevin was here," Jerusha told her, hopping down from the fence with a flounce of her skirts.

"Uncle Kevin is here, so get," he said, coming up just then in his unhurried way. Jerusha stuck her tongue out at him then gave him a ravishing smile as she and Sorrel trotted off. Brynn went on stroking Angelina's face, but she felt desperately uncomfortable. "Hello, Brynnlin," he said mildly, leaning beside her on the fence.

"Hello," she returned.

"Looks like a good turn-out, anyway," he observed. "Angy looks mighty good. Been busy with her, I see."

"Yes, sir," Brynn said. "Me and Jimbo did both horses this morning. He did Israel."

"Well done," her uncle told her. There was a pause, then he added: "Got something for you. From Adam."

He didn't see her surprised look; he was pulling it out of his inside jacket pocket. Then he did gaze down at her and she could see it. She could see that he knew it all and she felt the heat begin in her face.

"He left for Duggansville yesterday, Brynn," he said and his voice was still the same as it had always been, only a little kinder. "He—um—he said that he didn't want to see any of you up at Old House before he left, but that he wanted me to give you this." He held out the envelope to her and she took it tentatively.

He didn't say any of the rest of it, of course. He didn't say how his son had come to see him out at the field where he had been working and taken him aside, then they had walked awhile and talked. Kevin could see at once that something was up and had taken them some distance away from Buck and Taylor, although it was in the middle of a work day.

"Pa, I did something really stupid," Adam had told him. "I mean, really stupid. And I'm going to go to Duggansville to try to see if there's anything to be salvaged from my marriage. And to see Gid. I got to see Gid. I've got to **be** with Gid. I can't stand to be away from him."

"I see," his father had said.

"No, Pa, you don't," Adam had told him. "I did something I swore I would never do. I swore I wouldn't, and then I went ahead and did it anyway. I can't believe I did, but I did."

"Oh, Lord," Kevin said. "You didn't…"

"We didn't plan it," the boy looked so upset, he felt for him. "Neither of us, Pa, honest."

"You and Brynnie."

He nodded. "Yes, sir. She came by to tell me about the foreclosure on Old House---I think she had just found out about it---she was upset, I had been drinking; not that I was so drunk out of my mind that I didn't know what I was doing, I'm not saying that---but, anyway, one thing led to another and…."

"You don't have to spell it out for me," Kevin had told him. "I get the picture. Lord, Adam. We talked about this over and over…"

"I know we have," he replied.

"She's just a child…"

"No, Pa, she isn't," he said. "Believe me."

"Well, be that as it may," his father said hurriedly. "You know…"

"Yes, Pa, I know," Adam replied. "That's why I'm going. She told me to, anyway."

"Brynn did?"

"Yes, she did. She told me I'm still in love with my wife. And I'm think she may be right. Maybe. Whatever, though, I owe it to Gid to give it a try. So, I'm going."

"He left yesterday morning," Kevin told her. She was holding the letter, her eyes on it in her hand, but then she looked up at him and he saw the tears there.

"I'm sorry, Kevin," she said and her voice was so young. "I'm so sorry."

He sighed and pulled her against him. "Don't be sorry, girlie," he told her. "For Pete's sake. He told me all about it and I love you just the same. And he told me you sent him on his way and that's exactly what you should have done. Don't be sorry."

He didn't say that Adam had also told him that he would be back. Of course, Kevin knew he would be, at least to visit, but that was not what Adam had meant and Kevin knew that, too. Despite all that Kevin had said to him, Adam insisted that he still had unfinished business with Brynn.

Brynn,

I'm doing like you told me. See, I can be good sometimes. I'm leaving and going back to Bethy, but I'll be back your way one day. Wait and see. If I did anything to hurt you, I'm sorry, but I'm not sorry about what we did. I can't be sorry for that. And, no matter what you say, I know you're not sorry, either. It was too good. So don't go trying to fool me about that. I hope everything works out with Old House. If anybody can make it work, you and Boone can. Tell everybody bye for me. Remember how I feel about you.

Adam

She folded the letter back down and put it back into its envelope. She was some little way away from the paddocks, where she had walked when Kevin left her. She wiped her face and folded even the envelope over and shoved it into the pocket of her riding skirt. She decided right then that she loved her Uncle Kevin beyond words. Then, there was a movement out of the corner of her eye and she saw that they were leading Israel and Angelina out of their paddock and the time had come.

"She looks good," said the voice at her ear and she jumped.

It was Stephen Darcy. He was setting up a camera on a stand, the black cloth flapping in the small breeze. He smiled at her.

"That's your horse, yes?" he said. He was dressed in a shirt and tie and was pulling out a little pad of paper and pencil in a businesslike way. "I'm here in official capacity," he added. "The spring auction is worth reporting; people are interested in it. Your horse, the Appaloosa, isn't it? You ride it to my grandmother's."

Brynn hugged her arms about herself. She didn't want to talk. "Yes," she replied.

"How you going to get around if you sell her?"

"I don't know."

Stephen looked at her and put his paper away. "Heard about the problem y'all are having," he said. She looked at him quickly. "Well," he said. "Nothing much goes unnoticed in this town. Don't worry. I'm no gossip."

She dredged up a smile. "Just a newspaperman."

"That's different. What are you going to do, though? Selling your horses leaves you afoot."

"Stefan," she said and just managed to keep the shake out of her voice. "I don't want to talk right now. All right?"

He was silent, then said quietly: "I did take it upon myself to tell one person. What is it they say: 'Don't let your heart be troubled.' Isn't that what they say?"

Brynn was puzzled. "That's scripture."

"Is it? Well, all the more reason for me to say it."

When Stephen had left, she stood over to the side, back a little way from the crowd near where Boone was and after awhile, she realized that Jordan was with them, and then that Jerusha and Sorrel were there, too. They were all there together, like a flock of chickens, she thought fleetingly as Angelina was led out and walked up and down in front of the crowd.

A murmur went around the people as she was led past them; a few men put their heads together and looked at the papers they held as the auctioneer began his spiel.

"Now, ladies and gentlemen," he said in his voice that could carry to the outskirts of the crowd. "This here is a ten-year-old mare, Appaloosa as you can see, owned by the McKenna farms. You all know the McKenna horses. They've all been proved to be fine, healthy, well-trained and well-bred. This mare's never been bred, she's broke to harness or saddle, gentle as a woman. Look at the movement, ladies and gentlemen. Look at the muscle-tone. A baby could walk underneath her and she won't shy. We'll start the bidding at fifty dollars...."

"Fifty?" Jordan hissed in Brynn's ear. "He oughta start at hundred and fifty, at least. We won't get nothing."

"Shhh," she told him.

"He knows what he's doing," Boone told them. "Start off slow, get a bidding war going."

"Maybe nobody'll buy her and we can keep her," Sorrel said with a bounce.

They were bidding already, however. It was up to one twenty-five. Brynn gripped her hands together and thought that she would faint if they didn't hurry up. After it got up to one-seventy-five she took hold of Boone's sleeve and twisted it in her fingers.

"One seventy-five one seventy-five one eighty, thank you, sir. One eighty, one eighty, one eighty; one ninety to the man in the red shirt. One ninety, ladies and gentlemen.

One ninety, one ninety, one ninety---two hundred. Two hundred now. Two hundred two hundred two hundred. Do I have two twenty-five? Two twenty-five, anyone? Two ten, thank you, sir. Two ten two ten two ten. Come now, ladies and gentlemen, look at that movement in that mare. Two ten all it's going to be? Two ten two ten two ten…"

"We're not going to get near enough," Brynn murmured at Boone's shoulder. "Maybe Israel will bring more, though. But if Angy won't…."

"Seven hundred dollars," came the clear voice from somewhere. "In cash."

There was a gasp from the crowd, followed by a buzz and a unanimous turning of heads and craning of necks. The voice had stopped the auctioneer in mid-air. Brynn felt the air rush out of her.

"Well," the auctioneer said, stammering a little. "Well. You heard the bid, ladies and gentlemen. Seven hundred dollars has been bid for the Appaloosa mare. You did say **seven** hundred dollars, didn't you, sir?"

"Yes, I did," the voice replied.

"Who is it?" Sorrel asked hopping up and down to try to see.

"I don't know," Boone replied, and he sounded like Brynn felt. "I can't tell."

"So, the bid is seven hundred dollars," the auctioneer went on and picked up his gavel. "Are there any other bids? Are there any other bids past the seven hundred dollars offered? Any other bids, ladies and gentlemen?"

The crowd was still buzzing and now it was moving apart a little for whoever it was to make his way through. Brynn kept moving around, but she could only see the top of a hat moving. Beside her, Jordan gave a funny little sound and said:

"Holy smoke. It's Jackson Flynn."

She still couldn't see, but Boone said on her other side: "Holy smoke, it is Jackson Flynn."

And then he stepped to the front of the crowd and she could see his fringed jacket and his hat and his fringed boots and it was Jackson Flynn as big as life.

"Good God," Clay said, suddenly appearing at Boone's side. "That's ole Jack Flynn, ain't it?"

"Seven hundred is the bid, ladies and gentlemen," the auctioneer roared with a flair, his gavel in the air. "Any other bids? All out, ladies and gentlemen? Seven hundred it is. Seven hundred going once---going twice---." They were all holding their breath. "Gone!" he said and brought the gavel down. "Sold! To the trapper there in the front!"

There was a whoop of applause from the crowd, Jerusha jumped into Boone's arms and Sorrel into Clay's. Brynn stared straight ahead and, after a moment, when he could stop shaking hands with people, Jackson Flynn met her gaze and then he tipped his hat to her.

From across the crowd, Stephen came out from under his camera's cloth, straightened and nodded, smiling.

Boone went straight and took Israel off the register to be sold.

Jackson signed some papers and received the bill of sale for Angelina.

The clerk of the auction handed Brynn a bank draft for seven hundred dollars which she handed to her Uncle Kevin to put in the safe at New House until he could take it to the bank on Monday morning.

Jerusha and Sorrel asked if they could go to New House for supper and spend the night and, to their surprise, Brynn said that they could. Her Aunt Janny looked surprised, then pleased and asked if Brynn and Jordan wanted to come to---or just to supper---or whatever.

Brynn looked at Jordan and said for him to go on. He asked if she was sure and she said sure she was sure.

Boone was already over at where the Carson horses were

talking to Schuyler, so Janny said she wouldn't bother to ask him, but wouldn't Brynn come too?

"To tell you the truth, Aunt Janny," Brynn said. "It would be sort of fun to be by myself up at Old House this evening. Is that all right?" she added, rather anxiously. She really didn't want to disappoint her, all of a sudden. She knew she had disappointed her a lot lately.

Her aunt had smiled and said that was fine and they would see her in church in the morning. Brynn breathed a sigh of relief on so many levels, she wasn't sure which one was the best.

And then, she found herself leading Angelina out to crop the new spring grass a little way from the rest of the people. Just about that same time, Jackson came strolling up and they found themselves comparatively alone. Brynn stood holding the lead, Angelina grazing down around the toes of her boots with comfortable tearing sounds, and after a moment, she handed the end of the lead to him.

"Thank you," she said.

He took it and asked: "For what?"

"For seven hundred dollars. In cash."

"I got a good mare out of it," he said. "Fair deal."

"You could've got her for a lot less than that," she reminded him.

"Still a fair deal," he replied.

It was turning into a warm, blithely spring day. The wind coming down off the hills was still cool, but the sky domed above them in robin's egg blue with just the merest spikes of mare's tails, and the sunshine poured down. Brynn pushed the few stray strands of hair back off her face. He was looking down at the horse, then he looked at her and added:

"I do have a favor to ask of you, though."

"A favor? What is it?"

"Well," he said, the fringes on his jacket swinging gently in the wind. "when I go up into the hills trapping, or hunting or---anything, I don't really want to take her with me."

"Angy? You don't? Why not?"

"I go through some pretty rough country," he said. "I don't want to wear her out taking her up there. It wouldn't be good for her. So, I was wondering, if when I go, could I leave her with you. At Old House."

Of course, he hadn't thought she would object to that, but it was nice to see her face light up. "Leave her with us? You sure? I mean…"

"I'll pay for her keep, of course."

"No, you will not pay for her keep," she told him.

"Yes, I will."

"Jackson, no you won't," she said and that smile came full force. "For Pete's sake. Angy's family. We don't take pay for family. We'd be happy to keep her for you."

"And make sure she gets exercised, you know," he couldn't help smiling back at her.

"Exercised."

"Yes, well, she'll need to be ridden."

"Oh, I see."

"I think probably into town to Mrs. Darcy's and back every day while I'm gone would be good for her, then maybe some riding around extra wouldn't hurt."

"No, I'm sure it wouldn't," Brynn replied. "We'll be sure and do that. That is, if you'll do something for me, Mr. Flynn."

"Of course, Miss McKenna."

"If you'll come out and have supper with us again sometime soon. Would you?"

"Out to Old House?"

"Yes, sir. Would you?"

"I'd like to very much, Miss McKenna."

"Good."

"Well, well," Janine said to Kevin. They were standing together watching the next sale and she had to pluck his elbow a time or two to get him to look where she was looking. "What do you think of that, then?"

Kevin took his eyes off the team of bays long enough to look toward the pair with the gray mare, then took a second look. They were standing all alone out on the violently green grass, the wind blowing Brynn's dark hair around, the sun glinting off the chain of her locket about her neck, and they were smiling at each other. Jackson Flynn was saying something to make her laugh.

"I think my brother would go over there and break that up," he remarked.

Janine raised an eyebrow. "I think if that brother of yours knew the alternative, he wouldn't," she replied.

"Maybe that's true," Kevin allowed.

"He wants to marry her," Clay said, stepping up beside his parents at that moment. They both looked at him in surprise. He was eating boiled peanuts from the damp brown paper bag he carried and he nodded. "It's true," he said.

"How do you know that?" his father demanded of him.

Clay rolled his eyes. "Come on, Pa," he said. "You know it as well as I do. All you got to do is look at him." He strolled away toward where Buck and Kate were letting their children climb on the fence and stroke the colts for sale.

Both Kevin and Janine looked back at the couple with the mare, then Janny said: "He may have a point, husband."

Kevin sighed. "And what would Morgan say to that?"

Janine shook her head. "I don't know."

At last, when it was near noon, Brynn decided she would take herself home. Kate had asked her to come eat picnic with her and Buck and the children, but she had washing to do and a whole empty house to do it in and she told her no. So, she took Israel and rode toward home, thinking that, really, heaven couldn't be much better than the way things were right now.

    Happy ending, she thought. Except, of course, this isn't the end of anything, really. It's just an interlude, as Jerusha would put it. A respite. A breather. A happy breather, that would be more like it. She didn't care, really, what you would call it; she decided that she would just take it and enjoy it. So, she punched Israel into a slow canter away from the fairgrounds toward Old House, letting the wind flow through her hair. When she had gone a little way, she heard a shout and, turning in the saddle, she slowed the old horse so that Boone could catch up.

    "Where're you going?" he asked, letting Roanoke fall into step beside them.

    "Home."

    "How come? Kate's got fried chicken."

    "I know. I just want to get home. There's things to get done at Old House."

    Boone looked irritated. "There's always things to get done at Old House. If you worked all day and all night for a week, you couldn't get all the things done that need to get done at Old House."

    "I know. But, with the children away, I'll have more time to get it done."

    "And less help."

    "They don't help that much. Anyway, I like being alone sometimes. Don't you?" she looked across at him and he could see then that she was all right.

    He relaxed. "I guess. The children are all staying the night down at Kevin's."

    "I know."

    "I'm going to take supper over at Carson's."

    "Good for you."

    "I may be late."

"So? I don't wait up for you," she said.

"You'll be by yourself all evening."

She laughed at him. "Oh dear, I really don't know what I'll do with myself." Then, at his face she added: "It all **right**, Boonie. I'll be fine for one evening, for Pete's sake. I'll have Tommy Cat, anyway. I'll love it, in fact."

"You will?"

"Yes! Of course I will. Hey," she said. "You really getting cozy with Schuyler Carson's family, aren't you?"

He shrugged. "I don't know if you'd say that. I'm cozy with Schuyler Carson, though."

"Is that so?"

"Yep," he smiled. "I'm going to marry that girl."

"You what!"

"Don't look so horrified," he told her. "Not any time soon. Just someday."

She settled back. "Oh. Really."

"Had you scared, didn't I?" he grinned.

"Just remember you have responsibilities."

"Yes, mother, I know. But the responsibilities don't go on forever, you know."

"Well, they go on till Rue gets in school and the taxes get paid, at least."

"Yes, I know." He reined in and she did the same, letting the horses blow. "And so Jackson Flynn came riding in and saved the day again, didn't he?"

"Again?" she asked. She looped the reins and reached back to untie her hair, then, holding the loop in her teeth, began tying it back again. "When has Jackson Flynn ever saved the day?"

"Oh, well let's see," Boone said. "Just when he dragged you out of the tavern and took you to his place about five years ago, and got popped in the mouth by Adam for his trouble. Just when he ran into Long Barn when it was on fire and dragged you out of that. Just when he dragged me out of the tavern that other time, that makes how many?"

"I didn't know about the dragging you out of the tavern," she said with interest. "When was that then?"

"Never you mind," he told her. "That was just to make a point. Jack seems to be intent on saving us from ourselves, doesn't he?"

"Seems he does do a fair amount of dragging us around, it's true," Brynn admitted. "Anyway, that's done for this time. And I'm going. You run along and go to Schuyler's and have a good time. I've got things to do. Without anybody else around." Suddenly the sky and the wind and the cosmic-green grass was all just a little too much and, flinging her arms out to embrace it all, she sang: "It's spring, Boonie! Don't you love it? It's spring and we made it through the winter!"

"We haven't made it through six months, yet, though," he replied, catching Roanoke from shying away from her. Israel merely swiveled an ear back and then forward again. "Kevin said he'd give us six months. Just remember that. That'll be the fall."

"I don't care," Brynn said, hugging herself, her face to the sky. "Right now is right now and I'm going to have a good time. So you just go on to Schuyler Carson."

"Good time," Boone repeated, kicking his horse into a trot. "Have yourself just a high old time washing clothes, then."

She waved to him and he saw her go toward home at Israel's heavy canter for a moment before he turned Roanoke toward the river. He took a quick detour past Elisha's grave, but didn't dismount there. He just pulled his horse to a stop a moment, before riding on.

Brynn coaxed Israel to canter all the way to Old House land, then walked him the last little way to cool him before letting him out in the paddock by the barn. She walked up the long slope to the house, then, under where the clothes line swung, she stopped and turned to face the sweep of land that ran down into New House pasture. It was a beautiful day. Unconsciously, her hand went to the locket on its chain as it hung around her neck.

"It's a beautiful day, isn't it?" she said.

END

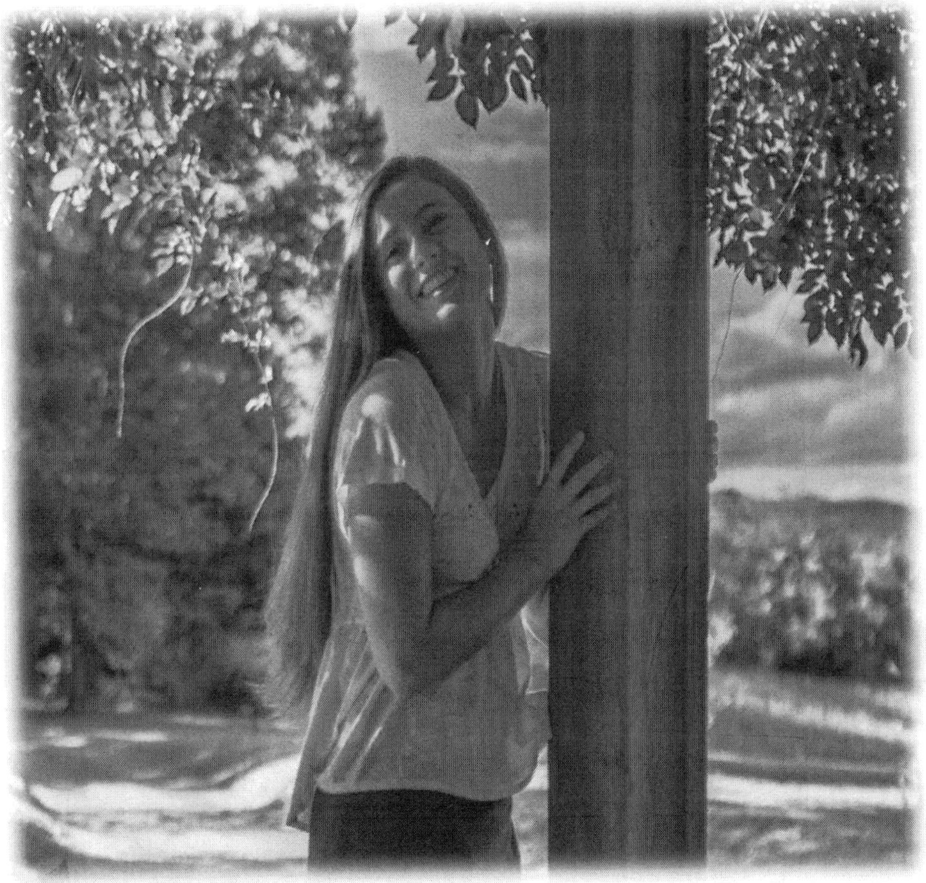

Made in the USA
San Bernardino, CA
23 November 2014